A FATAL ATTACHMENT

A FATAL ATTACHMENT

Robert Barnard

Thorndike Press • Thorndike, Maine

Library of Congress Cataloging in Publication Data:

Barnard, Robert.
A fatal attachment / Robert Barnard.
p. cm.
ISBN 1-56054-577-1 (alk. paper : lg. print)
1. Large type books. I. Title.
[PR6052.A665F3   1992b]   92-34173
823'.914—dc20   CIP

This is a work of fiction. Names, characters, places, and incidents either are the product of the author's imagination or are used fictitiously. Any resemblance to events or persons, living or dead, is entirely coincidental.

Thorndike Large Print® Cloak & Dagger Series edition published in 1992 by arrangement with Charles Scribner's Sons.

Cover design by James B. Murray.

The tree indicium is a trademark of Thorndike Press.

This book is printed on acid-free, high opacity paper. ∞

A FATAL
ATTACHMENT

CHAPTER 1

"Thea?"

"Oh hello, Lydia."

"Lovely day, isn't it?"

"Really lovely. Summer here at last, I hope."

"I was wondering, dear, if Andrew will be going into Halifax today, or in the next day or two?"

"I imagine so . . . Yes, I'm sure he will."

"It's so unlike me, but I'm nearly out of paper. I did so many drafts of the assassination chapter last week that I got very low without noticing it."

"A ream of A4, then? I'll tell him."

"That's awfully kind. Any old stuff will do. And tell him I shan't need it before the week-end. Any news? Any letters?"

"Nothing of interest . . . Oh sorry — I forgot. I did have a letter from Maurice."

"Poor Maurice. No sign of life on that front?"

"That depends what you mean by life, Lydia. The letter is full of details of in-fighting among the various television companies. I couldn't really follow it. I gather things are fraught because of the new Broadcasting Act."

"I know you think me a snob, Thea, but I can't get over the feeling that television is frightfully *infra dig,* and *commercial* television — well, almost beneath contempt."

"It's an old-fashioned view, Lydia. I get a great deal of cachet having a son in television, I can tell you, and I'd get a great deal more if he actually appeared on the screen."

"Most of my views are old-fashioned, I suppose. . . . When I said signs of life I meant that wife of his. Any signs of his getting rid of her yet?"

"No, of course not. He still seems quite devoted."

"Hmmm. He'll never be anything with that woman dragging him down. If only Gavin had lived. . . ."

There was silence at the other end.

"Well, thank Andy in advance. I'll drop down and pick up the paper when I know he's been into town."

"No need. He'll drop it up to you, or I will."

"Sweet of you, dear. You know I appreciate it. Have a nice day, as the Americans say."

"You too, Lydia."

Thus went the telephone conversation between Lydia Perceval and her sister Thea Hoddle on a morning in late June. Like most conversations, particularly conversations between near relatives, this one had not only a text, but a sub-text. Two sub-texts in fact. In Lydia Perceval's mind the sub-text went: I'll go through the motions of asking, but of course Andy will be going into Halifax, and we both know why. Maurice is a poor fish, pulled down by a silly job and an impossible wife, and he is so because you and Andy hated the influence I had over him. Not that Maurice had the seeds of greatness in him. But Gavin did. Gavin would have been a hero.

And in Thea Hoddle's mind the sub-text went: You know damned well Andy will be going into Halifax, because he has to collect his dole money and he has to buy drink. If Maurice's life is unsatisfactory it is because you had absurd ambitions for him and put absurd notions into his head. You fought me for my sons, you bitch. Gavin would never have joined the navy if it hadn't been for the nonsense you filled him with. You killed him! You killed my son!

Lydia Perceval finished a paragraph in her elegant, sloping longhand that could have been sent straight to the printer, so legible was it. She laid down her pen and stretched her arms above her head. A good paragraph in a good chapter. Craftsmanship was its own reward.

You felt good because you knew it was *right* — not right historically, though Lydia's use of sources was impeccable and her judgment balanced, but right artistically: the book would be shapely, aesthetically satisfying.

She got up from her desk and looked out of the window that gave on to the front garden. Summer really had come: the first roses were out, pink and triumphant. The laburnum was a picture — a shower of gold. No, *yellow*. Wordsworth was wrong about daffodils: they are yellow, and so is laburnum. Accuracy in all things, that was what Lydia believed in, though she did not always realize that understanding yourself and your own motives is often more difficult than understanding an historical figure.

She came from the window and walked around her study. Her eyes caught with affection the photographs and reproductions that she cherished: Queen Charlotte and her dog by Breeley, T. E. Lawrence on a motorcycle, George V and Nicholas II at Cowes, Byron landing from a boat in a rocky landscape, from the painting by George Sanders. At moments of stasis such as this she had always in the past had a cigarette. She had given them up three years ago, feeling nicotine was really a smelly menace and a weakness she could conquer, and she had. Still, nothing quite replaced a cigarette as something to *do,* in the intervals of writing.

Her eye strayed to the photograph on top of the little bookcase by the door, the photograph that was above all others painfully dear to her: her nephew Gavin in the uniform of a Royal Navy lieutenant, taken just a month before he set sail for the Falklands. He had been in Washington at the time, attached to the Embassy. He had written to her constantly about his job, his plans, his new and exciting friends. She had loved thinking about him, and the conquests he must be making. In the studio portrait he looked straight ahead at the photographer, clean, proud, brave. Her heart missed a beat as a picture came into her mind of the boys as she remembered them best: in summer shorts and shirts, wheeling their bikes up the hill from the village, Gavin dark and clear-eyed, the perfect sporting schoolboy, Maurice fairer of hair and smaller, but talking animatedly and excitedly. Then they would come in through her gate, and the lovely part of the day would begin.

And now Maurice was working at a foolish, demeaning job, married to a sluttish woman with a Birmingham accent. And Gavin, dear, dear Gavin, had sailed off, proud and excited, to fight in the Falklands War, never to come back.

She turned her eyes away from the photograph. It had always absurdly hurt her that her sister Thea had the same photograph on her living room mantelpiece. She went into her sister's home as seldom as she decently could.

She turned back towards her desk. Her biography of Charles X was reaching its climactic point: Louis XVIII would shortly shuffle off the long sickness of his life, and the old reactionary would become king at last. People with power, and the way they wielded it, had always fascinated Lydia. Her biography of Charles had not disguised her subject's weaknesses: his garrulity, his unwisdom, his treachery. And yet when it came to that moment when the last legitimate monarch of France abdicated on the steps of the Château of Saint Cloud, there would hang over her lucid prose an autumnal tinge of sadness and regret at a notable passing, a loss of much that was fine and beautiful.

She took a deep breath and sat down at her desk. Her next page was now clear in her mind.

Lunch was usually a scratch meal for Lydia. For dinner she cooked herself unusual and exquisite things, never thinking the effort wasted on herself alone, but for lunch she always had boiled eggs, or toasted cheese, or a made meal from Marks and Spencer's, kept in the deep freeze. Today it was canneloni, and when it was eaten, and a cup of tea drunk, Lydia was back in her study and looking through her morning's work, making minor corrections and putting question marks beside any statement that she felt might need verification. But before she got down to the afternoon's writing, she telephoned through to the British Library division at Boston Spa.

"Could I speak to Dorothy Eccles, please? . . . . Oh, Dorothy — Lydia Perceval here. I've got a list for you — is that all right? I'll be in on Monday the twelfth, all day. I have a whole mass of queries and problems to sort out. These are books and articles, and some of them will have to be got from London, I imagine. Ready? Right — here we go. . . ."

When she had gone through the list, spelling out the names of difficult authors, Lydia said:

"Do you expect to be busy that day?"

The rather breathless voice at the other end said: "I'm sure I could arrange not to be, if you needed help."

"Oh no. Everything on the list is pretty straightforward. I was thinking of lunch."

"Oh, that would be *lovely*."

"Slip into Wetherby, perhaps, to La Tavola Calda."

"Super."

"Well, barring any unpleasant surprises with the stuff you're getting out for me, it should be easy enough to take an hour or so off. So if you were able to get off, you could slip along to my desk, say around twelve o'clock."

"I *shall* look forward to that."

Lydia put down the phone. Dorothy Eccles was terribly useful to her, and it was good to repay her devotion. True, the work she did in a way repaid itself: she was flattered to work for a popular biographer whose books were at once respected by scholars and much read by book-buyers and book-borrowers — "both in this country and the States" she had once heard Dorothy say in hushed tones to one of her fellow librarians. Lydia had evidence enough that it warmed the little dried-up woman's soul to be part of the apparatus of scholarship and literature, and to be thanked in the acknowledgements section. She knew her feelings and enjoyed her devotion. It was right to reward it with some special treat now and then, and it did her own heart good to feel the woman's pleasure and excitement.

Suddenly a stab of feeling struck her to the heart: to be reduced to giving little treats to spinster librarians! She, whose life had once been so full, so happy, so fulfilled! What a deprivation, what an emotional barrenness had overtaken her, that she could give and take pleasure only on so meagre a scale! She put her head in her hands and tried for some seconds to regain her composure.

Then she shook herself and returned to her manuscript.

Some time after five she laid down her pen. The old king was not yet ready to die, but he was in the way of dying. Soon her man would be king, and she was looking forward to writing her account of his coronation — the last French coronation. She had a mass of material on the junketings that surrounded it, and she would enjoy marshalling it. She always watched the news at six, and then began preparations for dinner. Meanwhile the sun was streaming down outside, and the air was inviting. She pushed open the kitchen door and went into the garden.

The memories of Gavin and Maurice in the garden were mental pictures rather than plants. True, there was the Buff Beauty rose they had bought for her fortieth birthday — out now, and deliciously aromatic. But what she remembered was them working with her there: mowing the lawn and raking up the cuttings, forking and weeding, learning from her how to prune. And all the time talking — talking and laughing, talking about serious matters, about politics and their futures, talking, talking, talking.

She walked round to the front, where the garden stretched out towards the hill down to the village, gracious in its lawns and its roses. Was that greenfly? She looked closely. Yes, it was. And there were tell-tale black patches on a bud of one of her Mischiefs. She must get at them with a spray, or tell Hobson the next time he came. Hobson — he was all the help she had now, and very unsatisfactory and erratic help he was too. A cloud came over the sun, and suddenly she saw the garden as an image of its mistress: adrift, somehow bereft. It had had its heyday and was now past its prime. She wandered through it, her mind on the past — her own past, the boys', and mixed in with theirs the French nation's. She looked back at the house, its warm old stone glowing in the evening sun, and thought she must have a dinner party soon. The boys had been all the social life she had needed, and somehow after Gavin's death she had never created or got into any new social round. She walked under the yellow magnificence of the laburnum and rested on the gate. Ahead of her the rich farmland of the Dales stretched, dotted only with the occasional farmhouse or minor road. She turned her head to the right, to the hill that led down to the village, and her heart stopped.

Two boys, one fair and one dark, in shorts and summer shirts, were wheeling their bicycles up the hill.

CHAPTER 2

Andy Hoddle went to catch the bus into Halifax as soon as he had finished his breakfast. Nothing else to do. Nothing else to do most days, though he was conscious that, as an unemployed professional person, he ought to have plenty of interests, both intellectual and practical, with which to fill up his day. It was a question of being bothered to take them up. It was the same with breakfasts: Andy regretted the New Breakfast of fibrous cereal and brown toast, and he would have reverted to the old style if he could have been bothered to cook it, or persuaded Thea to. But he couldn't, so he just went along with the new dispensation. Because there was also the fact that sausages and bacon and eggs and mushrooms cost money. He and Thea had to save their pennies these days. Alcohol cost money too.

He had had the letter from the Department of Social Services two days before, and it was burning a hole in his pocket now. It had sounded ominous. Probably for that reason he had said nothing about it to Thea. As far as she was concerned this was one more day on the long, unsignposted road of his unemployment.

Of course once he got to Halifax there was nothing much to do there. He bought the ream of A4 for Lydia and immediately regretted it. Bloody heavy, typing paper — he'd forgotten that. He mooched around the shops, a balding, paunchy man in a suit that needed dry-cleaning. He bought himself a packet of ten cigarettes, and then made a systematic tour of the supermarkets, noting which ones had whisky on special offer, and which brands. He went to buy coley for their dinner, and got irritable with the fishmonger for trying to sell him too much. I'm becoming the typical pensioner, he thought: convinced that everyone is trying to swindle me.

It was eleven o'clock. Over an hour before his appointment at the Department. He ambled down to the Piece Hall, to sit in the central square, enjoy a cigarette and ease the weight of the paper. Bloody Lydia! She could have jumped into her car, fetched herself a ream of paper, and been home within the hour. Didn't even consider it, probably. Couldn't interrupt the great work of historical scholarship, no doubt. And Andy's got nothing to do, has he? He racked his brain to decide who she was writing about this time, but he couldn't remember.

Strange to think how happy they had been, the three of them, not so long back. Twenty-five years ago they'd been near-inseparable. It wasn't just the closeness of the sisters: he had been genuinely fond of Lydia himself then. Those wonderful holidays in France, year after year. Thea and Lydia had been Francophiles ever since they'd gone on exchange holidays there just after the war. As they toured around, first by train and bus, later by car, he had provided the bourdon of dissent: "The trouble with France is it's impossible to get a decent meal." "What do they call this wine? Château Clochemerle?" "If I want beautiful scenery I'll get it on the television, where it's always sunset and there's lovely music in the background." The self-conscious comic grouser, a role he had relished. His common touch had counterpointed Lydia's already rather middle-class persona. It had sometimes felt, then, as if he had married the two sisters, not just one.

Then the boys had grown too old and boisterous to be left with their grandparents, there had been Lydia's brief marriage — or was that earlier? Anyway, and crucially, there had been the fact that Lydia had started to . . . to *take the boys over*. There was no other way of describing it. And then Gavin had died, a ball of fire on the *Sir Galahad*, and since then Andy had somehow felt childless. Unfair to Maurice, but there it was — childless and empty. Redundancy had been no more than a confirmation of that emptiness, one more brutal kick at the expiring corpse of his happiness and self-esteem. Bloody Lydia! She had robbed them of their boy, and then killed him. And left him and Thea empty shells of their former selves.

He had a sudden vision of himself from the outside, as it might be any old layabout or drunk whiling away the day on a city bench, bemoaning his lack of the price of a pint, and compensating by mulling over all his ancient grievances.

He ground his cigarette stub angrily into the grass and got up.

It was still early for his appointment at (summons to, more like) the Department of Social Security. As he went out into the streets again he passed a pub with the doors open to let in the odd summer breeze. He could do with a drink. He looked in, caught the fug of beer fumes and tobacco smoke, heard the metallic chink of the fruit machine dispensing money to the mugs. Before he could turn into the Public Bar the juke-box started up, the bass charging into his head like a gang of football hooligans. He turned and went on his way. He didn't much like town pubs these days.

Only rarely went to his local village one, come to that. If a man's got to get stinking drunk, he said to Thea, he should have the decency to do it in the privacy of his own home.

He was lucky, really, that he could still say things like that to Thea — say them and laugh over them, say them without feeling shamefaced.

He was early at the D.S.S. Inevitably he was early. He sat around waiting with the other people who were early like him, other people who had nothing to do. Promptly at 12:10 he was called in to Mrs Wharton's office and found she was someone whom he had talked to briefly before: cool, down-to-earth, almost academic. He felt relieved. Like many another long-term unemployed person, he could cope with everything except sympathy.

She was a busy woman, and came straight to the point.

"You've probably read in the press that the government is clamping down on people claiming unemployment benefits in the upper-age group," she said, looking at him through large spectacles, grey-eyed, unsentimental. "This means they can no longer expect an automatic continuance of benefits, and are going to have to go on retraining courses to —"

"It's a con," broke in Andy Hoddle. "A

22

PR con to try and convince the public that people like me are shysters who don't want to work."

There was a pause, then a tiny smile from across the desk.

"Strictly off the record, and I'd deny it if quoted, I agree. For most people in your age group in this area the chances of finding a job are virtually zero. But not for all. Mr Hoddle, how long is it since you applied for a job?"

"Oh God, years, I'm afraid." He shook his head, unable to remember. "For about eighteen months or two years after I got the push I did, then . . . Well, it just got too depressing."

"Exactly. And I suppose you just applied for jobs in your own field?"

"Well, of course. I wasn't very likely to get one out of it, was I? I was an industrial physicist with Haynes, the electronics group. I thought in my naïveté that there were firms that would grab someone with my experience and expertise. Instead of which they went for the younger man every time — wet behind the ears, and with not an ounce of practical experience."

"It's the old story."

Andy shifted uncomfortably in his seat.

"I may not have put my best foot forward

in the interviews. I'd recently lost my son."

"I'm sorry. And are you over that now?"

"Yes . . . *No*. No, I'll never get over it. But to some extent I've put it behind me."

"Do you drink too much?"

Andy was under no illusions that it showed. He grinned, liking her a lot.

"What's too much? It depends on the person, on the circumstances — what you're trying to drown. Yes, I drink too much. A doctor would certainly say so."

"Would it impair your ability to do a job?"

"No, it wouldn't. A lot of it comes from the fact that I don't have enough to do. But as far as I'm concerned this job is a myth. If I couldn't get a job seven years ago, who's going to give me one now, when I've been out of the research field all that time?"

"The schools are crying out for science teachers."

"I am not a teacher."

Andy heard a sharpness in his own voice, and wondered whether it was caused by fear. Was it fear of failure as a teacher, fear of having a job at all? Unemployment robbed a man of confidence. He determined to pull himself together.

"The need is so desperate that the Department of Education is trying to attract people from outside teaching. There is a sort of on-the-job training and assessment programme."

"Flannel."

"Probably."

"Get in just anybody from the streets to massage the figures."

"Maybe. But you're not just anyone from the streets, are you? You're a well-qualified scientist with valuable experience. Do you think you could teach?"

Andy sat pondering, assessing himself.

"I don't know. I'm not trained. . . . I wouldn't want to let the children down."

"Or do you mean you wouldn't want to let yourself down?"

"I don't know. . . . The short answer is: yes, I do think I could teach."

"What makes you think so?"

"I used to coach my own boys. I've never had any problems with children."

Except that I lost my own, something screamed inside him.

"I feel strongly about this, you see," said Mrs Wharton, though still with her admirable coolness. "My own boy has had a succession of science teachers, all inadequate, and this is a subject that really interests him. I've been in touch with the local education people. There's a desperate need for someone at once at the North Radley High School."

Andy sat quiet for a moment.

"I need to think it over."

"I've been in touch with the head. He'll be in all afternoon."

"I'll have to think it over, I say."

"Do you know where North Radley High is?"

"I'll find it," said Andy.

When he left the D.S.S. he went into the nearest pub and bought himself lunch. Steak and mushroom pie and a half of bitter — just a few pence change out of four pounds. He realized that just by buying it he was committing himself to this teaching job. His small pension and the dole did not allow him to buy the most basic meal out as a rule — not with the amounts he spent on booze. He had quite unconsciously decided to take it. He was part of the workforce again. As he ate he realized that the reason he felt shell-shocked was that suddenly he was forced to think about the future. It was years since he had done that — years that had been consumed by mulling over the past. And now, suddenly, it seemed that life might change, that there might be new activities, new people. An interest in life, in short.

He found the North Radley High School without difficulty. It was in fact just off the bus-route home — a sixties building, the paint peeling off in the heat, but with quite a lot of bustle and laughter in its corridors and on its playing-field. The secretary said the headmaster would see him at once, and he was received with a friendliness that was tinged with gratitude and relief. The headmaster did not beg him to take the job, but Andy had the impression that if he had shown more reluctance, he would have.

"The lass who's been doing the job is three months pregnant, and she's been ordered to rest until the baby's due."

"There's only three or four more weeks of term," Andy pointed out.

"That's right — and a hell of a lot to cram into them. Starting now would enable you to settle in, so that both sides could see if it suited. If it went well, there'd be a job till Christmas and beyond. I may say, in confidence of course, that the lass herself is no whiz-kid. Had two stabs at her degree — that's why she's only had the lower forms. I'd guess that whether she decides to come back at all will depend on the mortgage rate at the end of the year. I've got a note from her here of what she's done with the various forms, and copies of the syllabus."

He handed them to Andy, who took his time going through them carefully, feeling an odd sense of power.

"Child's play," he said finally.

"Not to the children," the head said warningly. "Especially if they've not been too well taught. You'll not be able to take anything for granted."

"No, of course I realize that."

"We have reasonably good facilities, but one thing politicians and administrators never realize is that facilities are no use whatever if the teaching is poor. I think you could make a good teacher. What about you? Do you have that confidence in yourself?"

Andy Hoddle took a deep breath.

"Yes," he said. "Yes, I think I could do the job."

The headmaster took him round the school, showed him the labs, where classes were in session, showed him the classrooms and the staff common rooms. When asked if he could start on Monday Andy nodded as if it were the most matter-of-course thing in the world. The head said he'd go back to his office and put through the paperwork, and he shook Andy by the hand at the main door. Andy walked out into the playground with the unfamiliar feeling of being wanted. It almost made him light-headed. As he went towards the gate his step was buoyant: he had a job. He had something to do between nine and five. He had money coming in.

As he walked a bell rang and children started

coming out of school. He saw two boys, one fair and one dark, come out and make their way to the bicycle sheds. They looked straight at him as if they knew who he was, and he thought they must be boys from the village. As he waited at the bus stop for the next bus home they cycled past him on the long, winding road to Bly.

On the day that Lydia first saw the boys wheeling their bikes — the Tuesday — she did no more than smile and say "Isn't it lovely weather?" as they passed her. Lydia's cottage was on the brow of the hill, and they smiled back as they got on their cycles and rode on.

The next afternoon was slightly overcast, with a light breeze, but Lydia found some weeding to do in a part of the garden that jutted out towards the road and gave her a good view down the hill. When she saw two cyclists at the bottom of it she put down her trowel and went out on to the road to pick up some litter — two hamburger cartons, a cigarette-packet and several sweet-wrappings — that she had noticed there earlier.

"Aren't people awful?" she said to the boys as they passed. "You'd think they'd know better than just to throw things down in a beautiful spot like this."

The boys stopped.

29

"We did a project at our old school," said the younger of the two. "On recycling waste, and that sort of thing."

"That's important, of course," said Lydia, straightening up and smiling. "But what we really need is to teach people not to scatter litter in their wake. They don't do it in other countries. . . . Where do you come from?"

"Tipton. We moved a couple of months ago. We had a better school there than North Radley High."

Lydia was uncertain where Tipton was, and by the time she had thought of something else to say the elder boy had swung his leg over the bar of his bike and was riding off. The younger followed, smiling a farewell.

The next evening was more overcast still, and though Lydia stood in her bedroom for some time watching the hill road, the cyclists never appeared. At seven she gave up her watch and went and prepared her dinner.

Friday, the day of Andy Hoddle's appointment in Halifax, the hot steamy weather returned. Soon after the time when the schools were out Lydia finished work — which was going well, wonderfully well at the moment — and went out into the garden. She meditated wandering down to the village at around the time when the boys usually came up, but there was little in Bly except a pub she had not been in for years and five or six shops which she never nowadays used, so instead she decided to garden once more in the overhang where she could both see and be seen from the road. To her joy the fine weather brought the boys out again. As they approached her wheeling their bikes up the hill, wearing silky running shorts and bright sleeveless tops that Lydia felt rather regrettable, her heart nevertheless jumped in anticipation. She straightened up and waved casually.

"Where are you off to today?" she called.

The boys stopped on the road just below her, and the younger one smiled engagingly.

"The woods beyond the gravel pit. There's a clearing in the middle that makes a good racing track. We're aiming to win the Tour de France round about 1997."

"Shouldn't you be cycling up the hill, then? To strengthen your calf muscles or something?"

"We're keen but not that keen," said the elder boy. Lydia laughed.

"That's right. One should have priorities," she said.

"Do you have a nice garden?" asked the younger one.

"Quite nice. Not like the gardens in the South, but quite pretty. Why don't you come in and have a look?"

The boys nodded and, pulses racing, Lydia walked over the lawn to open the gate for them. They wheeled their bikes through, and Lydia pointed to an old stone seat let into the wall.

"That's where my nephews used to leave their cycles."

The boys took them over there, and then turned round to get a proper look at the garden. Lydia was pleased it was looking so fresh and green, like these two young lives.

"Gosh, it's lovely!" said the younger boy. "Do you have help with it?"

"Some," said Lydia. "The sort of help that's not much help, if you know what I mean."

"Our garden's all overgrown," said the elder. "Dad goes out there and makes a lot of noise, but he doesn't make much impression. The house was empty for six months before we moved in. Mum says she just hasn't the time or energy."

"Gardens need a lot of both," Lydia agreed.

"Are your nephews grown up now?" asked the younger.

"One is," said Lydia, turning momentarily away. "One was killed in the Falklands War, fighting for his country. The other is . . . in television, actually."

She was depressed to see their eyes light

up with interest.

"Does he appear on screen?" asked the elder.

"Nothing so . . . glamorous. He's deputy head of drama with Midlands Television, and he does a lot of scripts for one of their 'soaps' — *Waterloo Terrace.*"

She had put very definite inverted commas around the word "soap," but she realized the act of distancing would be lost on the boys. They, she could see, were enormously impressed by the mention of *Waterloo Terrace.*

"My mum can remember when she first saw television, can you imagine?" said the younger. "It was the queen's coronation. She says television was in its infancy then."

"It still is."

"Can you remember when you first saw it?"

"Yes, indeed. It was just after the war. We were down in London visiting relatives. They were showing off quite frightfully, because very few people had it then. I remember it was one of the Oscar Wilde plays. They had to have long intervals between the acts, to get the cameras from one studio set to another. I didn't think much of it then, and I don't think much of it now. But we haven't introduced ourselves yet. I'm Lydia Perceval."

"I'm Ted," said the elder boy.

"And I'm Colin."

"Ah. Ted and Colin — what?"

"Bellingham."

Lydia put her hand to her throat.

"Bellingham! My fate!"

"What do you mean?"

Lydia turned away, with a brief shake of the head.

"Nothing. I'm being silly. I'll tell you one day. You must come and have tea, and we can have a good talk."

The boys looked puzzled.

"Tea? You mean like a meal?"

"I mean afternoon tea, at four o'clock. With sandwiches and home-made cakes and scones. Don't look so puzzled. Everyone used to have it."

"We have homemade cakes and scones, now and then," said Ted. "But we sort of eat them on the wing."

"That's the trouble with today's world: no one takes the time and trouble to do things properly. Why don't we say tomorrow? I never do any writing at weekends."

"That would be great," said Colin. "Cakes and scones and jam?"

"Definitely cakes and scones and jam."

"Writing?" said Ted. "What did you mean, writing?"

"It's what I do for a living. I write people's lives."

"Gosh, fancy finding a writer stuck on top of a hill near Bly!" said Colin. He gave her his engaging grin, and then the two raised their hands in greeting and went to retrieve their bikes. As they rode off towards the gravel pit and the woods they raised their hands once more in farewell.

As she turned and went out of the sunlight into the cottage Lydia felt suffused by feelings of happiness such as she had not known in years, had almost forgotten, whose return she fervently welcomed.

CHAPTER 3

"We're going out to tea today, Mum."

"To what?"

"To tea. With Mrs Perceval."

All sorts of questions drifted into Dora Bellingham's mind: why Mrs Perceval should ask her sons to tea; why they had accepted; whether they would want anything later on. But she let them drift out again, and sank back into her chair.

"All right," she said.

The boys had discussed what they should wear for this unprecedented occasion in their lives, and they had eventually decided on grey flannel trousers, white shirts and school ties. When their father, hacking away randomly in their wilderness of a garden, saw them cycling off he came back into the house and stood in the French windows.

"Where were the boys off to?"

"They've gone out to tea."

"To *what?*"

"To tea with that woman they've been talking about. Lives at the top of the hill. Some kind of writer."

"What are they going out to tea with her for?"

"She asked them, I suppose."

"*Why* did she ask them? What is a writer doing, asking our sons out to tea? Didn't they say?"

"No. I didn't bother to ask."

He looked at her again, anger stronger than concern.

"You can't be bothered to do anything these days, can you, Dora? Come out for a meal with me. Come to the firm's parties. Have anyone for dinner, have anyone visit."

She could hardly raise the energy to protest.

"That's not fair, Nick. We had a visit from my mother just before we moved."

"Your mother coming isn't a visit, it's an Act of God."

Nick Bellingham stumped off angrily, back into the garden. He was not, in fact, particularly worried about his sons, but he was very aware that he was getting no support at a time when he was most in need of it. He was in a new job in a part of the country where he was made to feel a foreigner. He was manager of the Halifax branch of Forrester's, a TV and video chain store. It was the sort of business that had been badly hit by the current recession, and Bellingham was ever-conscious of the drastic dip in takings since he had taken over. He was also half-conscious that he had been appointed above his capacities, and this made him bluster. He knew that he needed back-up from his wife. Dammit, that was one of the things she was there for, wasn't it?

In the house Dora Bellingham sank back into her chair again. It was true, what Nick had said: everything these days seemed too big an effort. Nothing seemed *worth* doing any longer. Was it a reaction, after the move? Certainly that had taken it out of her. But she thought it had begun before that. She had been conscious that, though she loved her sons — of *course* she did — to do anything for them beyond feeding them and keeping them reasonably well turned-out was beyond her. She couldn't interest herself in their interests, let alone try to guide those interests. But that was all right, wasn't it? They were at an age when children naturally develop in their own way, grow away from their parents' influence. It was natural. It wasn't anything to worry about.

"I'd better take that ream of typing paper up to Lydia," said Thea Hoddle to her husband.

They were lying in deck chairs in the garden of their house in Bly. It was a substantial house, built in a style which Lydia referred to disparagingly as Headingley Tudor. It had been bought, of course, when Andy had a good job and a secure future. More recently they had taken in lodgers and the occasional bed and breakfast guest in order to make ends meet. Thea would be glad if those days were now over. At her time of life she no longer enjoyed sharing her home with others.

"Don't bother," said Andy, turning the page of his *Independent*. "I'll take it up to her this evening. I can then give Lydia the glad tidings that I am now in the ranks of the respectable and gainfully employed."

"Yes — I suppose you'll enjoy doing that," said Thea, looking at her husband affectionately. "Don't be mean to her."

"Mean to her? Why should you think I might be mean to her? We have always remained on excellent, cool terms. In any case I hardly have any sort of whip hand over her: I shall still be only a late starter in an ill-paid profession, and she will always be a successful and nationally known bitch."

"Do you think bitch is the right word to describe Lydia?"

"Witch, vampire, succuba, virago, harpy, vulture, bloodsucker, emotional leech — call her what you will," said Andy, waving his hand in a lordly way. "I haven't her skill with words."

"You manage," said his wife.

Lydia got great pleasure out of her preparations for tea. She had asked her cleaning lady, Mrs Kegan, to bring up a cake from the village baker's — she had given up making cakes years ago, and she didn't trust her hand now. But she made scones, and put them out with strawberry jam and cream, and she cut substantial sandwiches suitable for boys' appetites and filled them with cold beef, with tomato and cheese, with salmon and shrimp paste. These were the sandwiches that Gavin and Maurice had always called for, on the numerous occasions when she had fed them as boys.

It will not be the same, she kept telling herself. I must not expect it to be the same.

But the boys certainly did enjoy the same food. They arrived, nicely dressed but behaving rather awkwardly. It was the food that soon caused them to shed any gaucheness, and they tucked in with a will, Colin eating scone after scone and getting whipped cream all over his upper lip, Ted relishing the sandwiches. They probably would have preferred Coca-Cola to drink, but Lydia felt that on that there would be no concession: at tea one drank tea.

"Are you settling down at the new school — whatever its name is?" Lydia asked.

"North Radley High. It's all right," said Ted. "It's not a *good* school, but it's all right."

"Some of them laugh at our accents," said Colin. "But that's stupid. We don't have accents. They have accents."

"It helps that we're both good at cricket."

"Though there's some are jealous about that too. They say we'd never be eligible to play for Yorkshire."

"We say: 'Who'd want to?'"

Both boys laughed.

"I suppose it's helped that it's been such a lovely summer so far," said Lydia.

"Yes, it has," said Colin. "We're going away to the seaside when school breaks up. Southport or somewhere like that. Dad says if Mum can't make the effort we three men will go."

It was as if a door had opened a tiny chink, giving light on the situation in the Bellingham household. Lydia's eyelids flickered, but she was too clever to pursue the subject at once.

"I'm afraid I usually avoid the English seaside resorts," she said. "The English look their worst in warm weather: all those tattoos and hairy legs and beer bellies."

"And the men are even worse," said Ted.

The two boys rocked with laughter. Lydia smiled, then giggled indulgently. Nothing wrong with schoolboy humour. She would educate them out of it as time went by, into

41

something more refined, ironic. She had with Gavin and Maurice — though, heaven knew, Maurice could have no use for refined humour in *Waterloo Terrace*. Please God let these boys not disappoint her as Maurice had done.

"Does your mother not like the seaside?" she asked, her head bent over the teapot as she poured fresh cups of tea.

"Oh — it'd be the same if it was walking in the Lakes," said Ted. "Mum doesn't want to *do* anything these days."

"Probably her time of life," said Colin.

"She's only forty-four, you ignorant oaf."

"Well, you can get it early. Anyway, it's always been Dad who was the doer — always crashing around, digging and sawing and fixing things. Mum just lets things wash over her."

"Well, that's true, but you've got to admit it's got a lot worse lately." Ted turned to Lydia. "We think they'll get a divorce when we're grown up."

Lydia shook her head, though to her it sounded eminently likely.

"Oh, I'm sure you're exaggerating things."

"I don't think we are. Dad's getting more and more irritated. And he's not a patient person at the best of times."

"Did you divorce Mr Perceval, or did he die?" asked Colin, with schoolboy artlessness.

"His name was Loxton. I reverted to my maiden name. Actually we divorced."

"Why?"

"I didn't want to stay married to him any longer. Let's not talk about him. He's the original sleeping dog who should be let lie."

She said it with a smile, so that the boys should not feel abashed. Colin had not finished with questions.

"When I said our name was Bellingham yesterday, you said something funny — I don't remember what, but something about your fate. What did you mean?"

Lydia gave a gesture of dismissal with her hand and smiled charmingly.

"Oh, just one of my silly ideas. One of my ancestors was Spencer Perceval. He was the Prime Minister during the Napoleonic Wars, and he was assassinated in the lobby of the House of Commons by a man called Bellingham."

"Why?"

"He was a bankrupt who blamed the government. Actually he was probably mentally deranged, but they hanged him."

"Well, we're not mentally deranged," said Ted, smiling. "You needn't fear we'll assassinate you."

"I don't!" said Lydia.

"We're very ordinary really," Ted went on

apologetically, as if he sensed that somehow they had aroused excessive expectations. "We go to a very ordinary school — do nice safe things like cycling and playing cricket."

"Oh — safety," said Lydia dismissively. "Safety isn't something to live your life by — you'll find that out as you grow older. Anyway I'm not sure it's so very safe playing cricket. One of our heirs to the throne got killed by a cricket ball."

"Really?" said the boys together. "Who?"

"Frederick, Prince of Wales, son of George II." She ventured on a joke that Gavin and Maurice had always enjoyed. "His father died on the lavatory seat, and he died playing cricket. Which shows the Hanoverians gradually becoming less Germanic and more English."

The boys laughed unrestrainedly, Lydia with them. The concession to schoolboy humour had gone down well. She pressed more cake on them and felt a great wave of happiness surge through her. Her life was coming back into kilter again.

Trudging up the hill from Bly with a ream of paper under his arm, Andy Hoddle's eye was caught by two cyclists at the top. They seemed to be coming out of Lydia's gate. As they got on their cycles he saw them wave.

44

They passed him cycling on their brakes down the hill, and he recognised the two boys he had seen at North Radley High. He smiled at them, and they smiled back in a rather off-hand way. But then why should they pay him any attention? A balding man in late middle-age, running to fat, shabbily dressed. He wouldn't pay him any attention himself.

When Lydia answered his ring on the door-bell he sensed that she was flurried, and that she was reluctant to ask him in. Still, she could hardly leave him on the doorstep while she fetched the money for the paper: Lydia always did the right thing.

"Well, you have had a party," he said, in what he hoped was a neutral voice, as they stepped into the sitting room. "Looks like a prep school tea."

"Just two young friends. But they're older than prep school age."

"Yes they are."

Lydia busied herself with her purse to ease the silence.

"How much was it?"

"Just two ninety-five. I got the duplicating paper — you say it serves its purpose, and it's so much cheaper."

"Quite right. Oh dear — I've only got a ten pound note and some small change. Have you got change?"

45

"Only small stuff. Never mind. It'll do when I see you next time."

"No, Andrew, I couldn't think of it. I'll raid the piggy bank. You know I've had one ever since . . . since the boys used to come up. And I've never opened it."

"Most of the coins will have ceased to be legal currency," said Andy brutally. "Don't worry about it, Lydia. There's no urgency. I've got a job."

"You've *what?*"

Lydia failed to keep out of her voice a note of outrage, as if his getting a job robbed her of one of her legitimate reasons for feeling superior to him. Andy had wrong-footed her again, and a shadow of annoyance passed over her face.

"I've got a job. Actually it's at North Radley High, where your new boys go."

Lydia, determined not to react to that, took to rummaging in her purse again.

"Oh, here's another pound. I think I can do it. Yes — do you mind all this small stuff? Well, that *is* good news, Andy. Do you think you'll enjoy teaching?"

"I think I'll cope. I used to coach Gavin and Maurice a lot with their physics, you remember. Oh, we had a phone call from Maurice, by the way. They're coming up on a visit the weekend after next. You must come down while they're here."

"They? Is that wife of his coming too?"

"Oh yes. And the baby."

"Well, perhaps — perhaps if you'd just ask him if he'd come up and see me. You'll think me snobbish, but I've tried and I *can't* like that woman."

"You've only met her once, Lydia. Perhaps you should try over a longer period. We shall, of course. Maurice obviously loves her. It's the least we can do."

"Ye-es."

"Particularly as Maurice always felt — I'm sure he felt — under the shadow of Gavin. Imagined he was less loved. Thea and I have always felt guilt about that."

Lydia always hated it when Thea or Andy talked about loving their sons.

"Gavin was so brilliant," she said assertively, as if staking a claim or rebutting a criticism. "It was impossible not to feel that he was special. If he had lived he would be enjoying the fruits of success now. Captain of his own ship . . ."

"Perhaps." A thought struck Andy, and suddenly it became impossible to keep it back. He shook off the restraints of all those years since Gavin's death and looked straight at Lydia. "The difference between us, Lydia, is that if we should hear tomorrow from a sur-

vivor that Gavin at the end behaved in a cowardly or a despicable way, I would love his
memory exactly as I do now. So would Thea.
But your love for him would be destroyed."

She looked at him with outrage.

"Cowardly? Gavin could never have behaved in a cowardly way. What a disgusting
thing to suggest."

Andy shook his head sadly.

"You see — you haven't got my point at
all. You didn't love Gavin as a person — and
that's true of Maurice too. You can't forgive
him for not being the sort of person you
thought he should be. But we can accept it,
and we'll try to accept his wife as well. Good
night, Lydia."

She could hardly bring herself to return his
farewell. He had done an unforgiveable thing:
he had dragged all the feelings about Gavin
and his death out into the open. Into the hideous, demeaning light of day. So far they had
all three of them nursed those feelings, nour-
ished them in private, and thus had managed
to keep up that facade of friendship and family
affection which propriety demanded. What
would come of that now?

And he had destroyed that feeling of warmth
and happiness that the visit of the boys had
brought her. Despicable. But, she told herself,
a failure like poor old Andy was bound to

be resentful of success, resentful of happiness. Bound to be a destroyer.

As he walked through Lydia's gate Andy felt glad he had brought things out into the open at last, and pleased that he had defined the difference between Lydia's love for his sons and his own. But as he walked on his mood changed: he began to feel mean and defiled. His love for Gavin did not need to be defined. And certainly it should not have been used to score a point over Lydia. Once again she had brought out the worst in him, had besmirched the finest, most pure emotion he had ever known.

Then he felt guilty that he could not feel so fine and pure a love for Maurice.

CHAPTER 4

"She likes us."

"Of course she likes us, you oaf. Goes out of her way to meet up with us, asks us to tea . . . It was good, that tea."

The boys had needed a couple of days to assimilate their first independent social occasion. Bicycling had precluded talking on the way home, and when they had got there they had walked in on a domestic row — or rather on their father shouting at their mother, and their mother looking as if she were a thousand miles away, examining some recherché fragment of Greek statuary, perhaps, or some intricate Byzantine mosaic. It had struck Ted suddenly at that moment that he hardly recognised his own mother.

Now, the Monday evening, when they were up in Ted's bedroom supposedly doing their English homework, they could talk about the experience because they had both thoroughly digested it. Ted, the elder, was a confident, sturdy boy, with a lock of dark brown hair falling over one eye. He should have been the one who could best understand the nature of the bond Lydia had begun to forge between

50

herself and them, but in fact this was an emotional area in which he felt uncertain. Perhaps this was because the bonds between the Bellingham boys and their own parents were ill-defined: semi-detached love from their mother, a hectoring, blundering concern from their father. Colin, slighter but handsomer, with a charm of which he sometimes revealed that he was aware, seemed to accept Lydia more whole-heartedly.

"She's very intelligent," he said now.

"Yes . . . She's more than that. A teacher can be intelligent. Lydia's an intellectual."

"What's the difference?"

"Well, it's like more so. I mean, an intellectual lives by his brain. His whole life is in the mind. He's always thinking."

"I don't think her whole life is in the mind. Otherwise she wouldn't be so interested in us."

"I don't mean it literally, daftie." Ted thought for a few moments. "She talks a lot about her nephews."

They both sat thinking about that for a time. The thought that they were in some way substitutes was both obvious yet difficult to put into words.

"At least she *does* take an interest," said Colin.

"Yes. It makes a change. . . . Though Dad's

interested, I suppose."

"Do you think so? When he's around he sometimes shouts at us. I suppose you could call that an interest."

"Mum used to be interested. . . . I'm worried about Mum."

"Yes. Something's happened to her. She's just switched off . . . Do you like her? Lydia, I mean."

Ted considered. He was a considering boy.

"Yes. Yes, I do. She's interesting. Out of the ordinary. She doesn't say the sort of things ordinary people say. And she doesn't talk down to us."

"She makes you think," agreed Colin. "Makes you see things from a different angle. . . . In a way it's flattering."

"Flattering?"

"That she seems so interested in us. It makes you think you're not so ordinary after all."

"You never did think you were ordinary," pointed out Ted, who knew his brother better than anyone. "You've got a very high opinion of yourself." He thought. "You know, I do wonder whether she'd be *as* interested if we were both girls."

They thought about this.

"I rather don't think she would."

"Don't let her hear you come out with

52

a sentence like that!" They both laughed. They could still look at Lydia with objectivity. "She has standards. That's rather good in a way. She . . . she has expectations of us."

"That's all very well," said Colin. "But what's in it for us?"

"Like I said, it's someone who's interested in us. It's like another home life — and we don't get much home life here. And Lydia's an education in herself."

Colin pursed his lips. He had meant by his question something much more concrete, but on reflection he decided to keep his own counsel. Colin, so apparently open and artless, was yet a lad who was very good at keeping his own counsel.

In Ted the interest in their burgeoning friendship with Lydia Perceval ran parallel with a concern for their mother. That evening, when she had dragged herself upstairs to yet another early bed, he said to his father:

"Dad, don't you think Mum may be ill?"

Nick Bellingham shook his head with the decisiveness that was characteristic of him, and which hid a congenital uncertainty.

"No. She's just exhausted after the move. She never wanted to move up here anyway. She's just getting back at me."

"Either she's exhausted or she's getting back at you," said Colin cockily.

"That's enough of your lip!" shouted Nick.

"I think you're wrong, Dad," said Ted. "I think it's physical. I think she should go and see a doctor."

"Crap!" said Nick, banging his hand on the arm of his chair. "There's nothing wrong with your mother. She should make an effort, snap out of it. Anyway, who's stopping her seeing a doctor?"

Nick Bellingham's air of decisiveness was in fact often a cover for the fact that he liked to keep all his options open and tried to face all possible directions at once. Ted silently decided that it was up to him to persuade his mother to see a doctor, because no one else would.

Andy Hoddle took to teaching like a duck to water, or so he told himself. His colleagues told him he was having an easy ride: end of term was near, the general atmosphere throughout the school was relaxed, and many of the kids he was teaching were aware there was a lot of catching-up to do. Andy found a way of mixing new material with a thoroughgoing revision of older stuff that did not imply a criticism of his pregnant predecessor. Inevitably there were the usual troublesome

54

children, the usual bored ones, but most of them he found bright and interested.

Andy thrived.

He did not see that a parents' evening presented him with any special problems. All the visitors would know that he was new, and would not expect him to have identified their Johnny or their Katey. In fact several of the parents made a point of coming up and saying that they hoped he would stay at the school as long as possible, that their Johnny or their Katey had been enthusiastic about their Physics class for the first time, that they hoped he realised there was a lot of groundwork still to cover, and so on and so on. It was all rather flattering, and made him feel wanted, made him feel he was doing a good job. He got on well with his new colleagues, which added to his confidence. They were the sort of hard-pressed, well-meaning people he could identify with, feel kinship with. One of them was giving him a lift home, and they were meeting up with Thea in The Wheatsheaf for a pint or two after the exhaustions of the evening.

It was late in the parents' evening when he was approached by Nick Bellingham.

"Would you be the new science teacher?"

"That's right," said Andy.

"Nick Bellingham's the name," he said, extending his hand. "I'd like to have a word about Ted and Colin."

"Ah."

The man sat down hard on the chair in front of Andy's desk, legs apart, and slapped his hands down on his thighs. Thus did industrial magnates behave in plays about the nineteenth-century North. Andy registered that he was watching a performance, but was unsure whether it was being put on from guile or from uncertainty.

"I've been very disappointed, to be frank with you, because they were both very interested in science back in Tipton — that's where we've come from — especially Ted. And, not to put too fine a point on it, it hasn't been maintained."

"Well," said Andy carefully, "it's always useful to identify someone with a special interest in the subject. Ted Bellingham, you said. He's in 4A, isn't he?"

Andy knew perfectly well who Ted Bellingham was, and which class he was in. He had put names and forms to Ted and Colin on his first day at North Radley High.

"That's right. We moved here a matter of months ago. I hear you're from Bly. Need a lift home?"

Andy involuntarily stiffened. So he was known not just to the boys but to their father. It was also known that he had no car. He tried to relax. There were several children from Bly at North Radley High. His reputation in the village was something he was going to have to live down.

"Thanks very much, but I'm fixed up for a lift. About Ted's interest in science —"

"Well, I wouldn't want to pretend he has any special aptitude. We'll hope he goes in that direction, but so far it's been mainly what you might call a practical bent. Engineer rather than scientist, if you get my meaning."

"I do, of course."

"They're not great brains, my Ted and Colin, but they're bright enough boys. Your sister-in-law has been good enough to take an interest in them this last week or so."

"Ah."

Andy was glad the man had brought the subject up, because if he hadn't he had certainly intended introducing it himself. He could not stand by and see what happened to him and Thea happen to another family.

"Good of her, as I say. Because their mother — I don't want to tell tales out of school, but it's the truth — she seems to have given up on them entirely. Move seems to have taken it out of her . . . or something. So Mrs Perceval's interest has made up for that. Some kind of writer, isn't she?"

"Lydia writes rather well-thought-of biographies. She —"

"Not really my boys' line, but her interest is much appreciated. Well, I'll not take up your time —"

"Mr Bellingham —" Andy put a restraining hand on his arm. "Lydia is a very intelligent woman, and probably well-meaning in her way, but she is rather dominating."

"Oh, I've no fear of them being dominated. My boys are just normal lads, but strong-minded in their way. If there's anything of that sort they'll just stop going. No, as I say, I'm grateful for the interest."

"I think you should take this seriously, Mr Bellingham. When I say dominating I don't mean that she would boss them around. I mean that she would dominate their lives. Lydia has no children of her own, and she does tend to take over other people's and edge out the real parents. I think you should warn their mother."

"Ah — if only I could! If only I could get through to her. But I'll keep my eye on things, Mr Hoddle, don't you fret. And keep my boys at it — hard work never killed anyone."

And he was gone with a raised hand. The man thinks in clichés, thought Andy bitterly. Well, if I can't warn the father, what can I do? Warn the boys? That would really lead to a bust-up with Lydia! And would the boys take notice of an elderly teacher with a drink problem, in preference to a sophisticated writer with a world reputation? They would smile and nod and do exactly as they felt like doing.

Later, in The Wheatsheaf with Thea and his colleague Angela Broadbent, he said:

"I tried to warn the father of the Bellingham boys about Lydia, but he didn't want to know."

"Is that Lydia Perceval?" asked Angela Broadbent, who taught history. "She's your sister-in-law, isn't she? Why should she be warned against?"

"She has no children of her own and she tends to take over other people's. Gradually she attaches them to herself, so that in the end there's nothing left for anybody else, not even the parents."

"But she's a good writer," protested Angela. "Absolutely reliable on facts. She must be an intelligent woman." She turned to Thea.

"Isn't Andy exaggerating a bit?"

"*No,*" said Thea.

That evening it was three days since Lydia had seen the boys. Too long, she felt! Not that she had any intention of exacting from them constant and unremitting attendance on her: that would have seemed to the outside

59

world, and to Lydia herself, unmanly and un-
natural. Still, she liked the sight of them, the
reassurance that they were still around.

When she was washing up, after the elegant
little dinner she had cooked for herself, she
heard through the open window shouts from
the road: the boys on their bicycles, going to
the wood to train. Were the shouts some kind
of signal to her, even an invitation? She smiled
indulgently: she was willing to be invited. She
pulled the plug from the sink and went to
fetch a cardigan.

At the door she paused, unusually uncertain.
Was it really an invitation? More likely it was
just one of them happening to shout at the
other. She went to fetch a basket, to gather
wild flowers in as an excuse, then she changed
her mind. She wasn't really a wild flower sort
of person, and she couldn't impersonate one
convincingly. She was, in flowers as in everything else, on the side of cultivation. And
writers didn't need an excuse for walking.
Writers need to think.

It was a ten minute walk to the wood, and
as she approached she heard the occasional
shout from the boys, and they lifted her spirit.
She knew where they would be. She took a
little path through the edge of the wood, and
came out on to the flat, sandy patch of open
land, with the gravel pit to one side of it, and

the wood to the other. The boys had worn a circle as they raced around it, and they were on their circuit now. Their heads were down, but Lydia was sure that Colin registered her as she emerged from the trees. They were in shorts and bright T-shirts, and they seemed to go faster and faster, spurred on by her presence. Each time they skirted the gravel pit they appeared to go closer, and her heart stopped, then beat faster in love and admiration: she admired people who took risks, scorned those who played safe. These were brave boys, she told herself contentedly: ones who would carve their own ways in life, not tread tamely in the ways of other people. Suddenly Colin waved to her, slowed down, and then jerked the front wheels of his cycle into the air and began a series of tricks, while Ted joined him and started doing the same. It was a weird sort of mating ritual, a peacock dance, and Lydia was enchanted: she smiled delightedly at their youthful high spirits.

Finally they stopped and wheeled their bikes over to her, sweaty, breathless, but still full of energy.

"Do you come here often?" Colin asked, in a parody of a music-hall comedian's voice. They all laughed.

"No, not often. But sometimes I like to walk and think in the evenings. About what I've written in the course of the day. About the next day's writing."

"Have you got a knotty problem?" asked Ted.

"Something like that. My man has just become king. I don't write the sort of biography where you imagine the subject's thoughts, but since there's no documentary evidence of how he felt on the occasion the temptation is there. I might succumb to a 'Perhaps he thought, perhaps he felt' paragraph, but I rather despise that kind of shift. Enough of my problems. What are you doing up here so late?"

"There's a parents' evening at school. Dad's gone. Mum's just mooning around. There's nothing much on the telly — not that I watch much anyway. So we came up here for a practice."

Lydia looked at Colin approvingly.

"Good idea. To my unpractised eye you both certainly seemed to be going well — really fast. Are there other sorts of training you have to do?"

"Oh, there are various sorts of weight-training," said Ted, shrugging. "Raising weights with the legs, to strengthen calf and thigh muscles. There's a gym in Halifax we go to now and then, when we've got the money."

"But we're not *that* serious," said Colin. "It's not our life's work, or anything."

"You're probably wise," said Lydia. "Sportsmen get burnt out so early, don't they? And then they have nothing left to do." She looked at them both, smiling encouragingly. "And what *is* to be your life's work?"

They grinned back.

"That's the question, isn't it?" said Colin. "The world's our oyster. Fame and fortune await us. That's what people always say to kids, but it rather ducks the main question: what are we going to get fame and fortune *in?*"

"The Air Force?" suggested Ted. "I rather fancy it."

"Engineering?" said Colin. "Some big project in the Third World?"

"You'd never find the Third World," said Ted. "Your geography's lousy. What about inventing something fantastic but simple, that will revolutionise everyone's daily life?"

"Most modern inventions have impaired the quality of life," said Lydia. "Made people lazier and more dependent."

"I bet you don't use a word-processor," said Ted, grinning.

"I do *not!*"

"Most people our age are thinking about going into computers," Colin pointed out. "You're sure of a job for life in the computer industry."

"All the more reason to avoid it! Go for something where *you* carve out your path, where you *make* people want to employ you — if you must be employed."

"Carving a path," said Colin. "What about the SAS?"

"Politics?"

"The diplomatic service?"

"Television?"

"*Not* television," said Lydia. They all laughed. Her heart was gladdened that they had not chosen, that neither of them at this early stage had his future mapped out. The world was all before them. She would be with them as their plans matured. She would help them map those futures out. She would not guide them, of course, but she would stimulate them.

Ted raised his hand.

"Must go. I'm trying to persuade Mum to go to the doctor's tomorrow."

"You haven't a hope," said Colin. "Irresistible force and immovable object. It will take days and days."

"So you really think your mother's . . . problem is medical, do you?" Lydia asked Ted.

"It must be. I don't see what else it could be."

"She wasn't . . . like this before?"

64

"No, she wasn't, was she, Colin?"

"Not so much so."

Lydia registered this further piece of disloyalty. It seemed that Ted did too. He turned his bike towards the road.

"Must go. See you soon."

"I hope so. Come and see me whenever you feel like it."

She watched them as they cycled erratically down the bumpy track. Then she set off after them. It was twilight now, and there was only the odd bird singing, but she felt very happy. When she got to the road she saw them already at the bottom of the hill, turning off to the village and home. She walked on in the cool of the evening, and barely a car passed her. When she got within sight of her cottage, however, she saw a car parked on the road outside, and as she approached it she saw it was a beetle. What an amusing little car that had been! You didn't see many of them about these days. She certainly didn't know anyone who still drove one.

A man was at her front door, just turning away, but stopping as he heard the click of the gate. He had a bushy black beard, and was dressed in check shirt and jeans. As Lydia approached she put on her best social smile and said:

"Yes?"

He looked down at her, a tiny smile playing around the corners of his lips. Lydia frowned, feeling she ought to know him. The man took pity on her embarrassment.

"Don't you recognise your husband, Lydia?"

CHAPTER 5

"Former husband," said Lydia briskly.

"Former husband," agreed the man.

"Well . . . You'd better come in, Jamie," said Lydia, and turned to open the door, glad for the chance to hide her face. Once inside she led the way through to the sitting room, went round turning on lights to gain time in her uncertainty, then asked, without welcome in her voice:

"Something to drink? It used to be beer, didn't it? But I suppose nowadays it's white wine, like everybody else."

He was standing there quietly, watching her, with a gentle, rather attractive smile on his face.

"If you could manage whisky with water that would be fine. Otherwise white wine, or whatever you've got."

Lydia could find nothing disparaging to imply about whisky and water, so she mixed one, glad of the opportunity to disappear into the kitchen. She got herself a gin and tonic at the same time, then handed Jamie his drink, gestured him to one of her capacious arm-chairs, and sat down herself.

"Well!" she said, looking at him.

"Have I changed so much since we were married," he asked, smiling, "that you didn't recognise me?"

Lydia had to bite back the reply that she hadn't recognised him not because he had changed but because he had made so little impression on her at the time. It would not have been true, but it would have been a very satisfying put-down.

"The beard," she said, waving a hand. "It certainly makes you look more . . . gives you a certain air."

"Makes me look more decisive," said Jamie, a smile playing round his barely visible lips. "Beards cover a multitude of weak chins — the comment has been made. No need to be tactful with me, Lydia. Though by the by I wonder how strength of character came to be seen to reside in a particular type of chin. It's rather unlikely, isn't it?"

"Rather," agreed Lydia. "Though these popular ideas usually have something in them." She was unwilling lightly to relinquish the correspondence between his chin and his nature. She now left a silence which said, as clearly as words would have: "To what do I owe the honour?"

"You'll be wondering why I came," said Jamie obediently.

"Yes."

"Well . . . I thought it was only fair to let you know that I'm back in the district."

"Oh."

"Yes." He shifted easily in his chair, his eye on her. It flashed through Lydia's brain that Jamie knew her as few other people did. "I've taken a lease on a small farm over Kedgely way. Organic vegetables, free-range hens, that sort of thing."

Kedgely was five miles or so away from Bly, by a winding hill road. The prospect of having her former husband so close was not pleasant to Lydia.

"Oh, it's farming now, is it?"

He smiled, untouched by her scorn.

"Yes, it's farming now. After the civil service, the City, local government, second-hand books, commercial travelling —"

"I haven't followed your . . . career," said Lydia, with another wave of her hand.

"My long succession of failures, you mean."

"You really don't have to apologise for them," said Lydia. "You are nothing to me . . . as I'm sure I am nothing to you."

The words seemed to be belied by the force with which she said them.

"I wasn't apologising," said Jamie, still genial and apparently imperturbable. "I was just getting in first, and trying to emphasize how right you were to leave me. Or to persuade me to leave you. It would never have worked out. I realized in the first week that you'd married me because you couldn't marry Robert."

A sharp expression of anger crossed Lydia's face. This was not the first time this had been said to her. Wanting to marry Robert Loxton was certainly a sign of greater discrimination than actually marrying Jamie Loxton. Still, acknowledgement of the truth of the analysis seemed to convict her of a double degree of foolishness. She left a couple of seconds' silence.

"Robert has certainly made himself *known*, done something with his life," she said cautiously.

"Oh, he has. When I tell people my name is Loxton they often ask if I'm related to him. When I say he's my brother the polite ones suppress their surprise."

"He's in Greenland — no, Alaska — at the moment, isn't he? I have an address somewhere to write to."

Jamie Loxton nodded.

"Alaska. Him and Walter Denning on a two-man survival expedition of some kind. No doubt it will prove something or other about the limits of man's endurance. Not something I've ever been very interested in, though I suppose my own survival proves something.

We write friendly letters once a year at Christmas, if he's around. I haven't seen him for — oh, five years or more. . . . He should have married you, Lydia. You would have made a fine pair."

Lydia could find no reply. She was remembering her childhood, and how vividly her elder Loxton cousin had figured in it. He and Jamie were the children of her mother's brother, and they lived over Malton way. In her early years — the war and its aftermath of austerity — they had seen each other perhaps once or twice a year, but what happy, golden times they had been. In the fifties they had come together much more often. Lydia's father was head of a mass-market clothing firm in Halifax, and British business appeared to be booming. Both families had cars, both groups of parents enjoyed each other's company. Now and then, in holiday times, Lydia and Thea, or Lydia alone, would take the train to Malton just for the joy of participating in the boys' games and projects. *Something* — something funny or adventurous, always with a spice of surprise or danger to it, or something to test their physical prowess — was always going on.

Perhaps she had understood then that the originator of these games was always Robert — that of the brothers one led and the other tagged along. Certainly by the time she had reached womanhood, had completed her degree and was out in the world, she had known that the one she wanted to marry was Robert. That had been the beginning of her going wrong emotionally. It had been some years before she realized that the projects and adventures of childhood had persisted into adulthood, and that Robert would be married to them and never to any woman. He was funny and affectionate and exciting when they met, but those meetings were always when he was just back from the Himalayas or shortly off to Antarctica or Siberia. So she had married Jamie when he had asked her. And in the few months of their marriage she had learnt the bitterest of lessons. She had never again settled for second best. Second best, she now knew, was coming nowhere. It humiliated her to think that she had needed to learn that lesson, and how she had learnt it.

"I don't think it's a good idea to marry a cousin," she said at last dismissively. "Royal families did it all too often. It weakened them in the long run. Much more sensible to seek out new blood."

Jamie nodded.

"As I gather Thea and Andy's boy has done," he said. "Do you see a lot of them?"

"Maurice and his wife? Oh no, of course

not. He's with Midlands Television — lives in Birmingham of all places."

"I meant Thea and Andy."

"Of course," Lydia lied. "They're here in the village. We see each other all the time."

"I must go down and call on them before long. I always thought Thea was the best of us."

"The best of us?"

"The kindest, nicest, most understanding."

"Well . . . perhaps you're right."

Lydia was reluctant to acknowledge Thea's moral stature, still more reluctant to acknowledge Jamie's right to make confident judgments. There was something more . . . more independent about Jamie now, and it disoriented Lydia. She was reminded of Robert more strongly than at any time since she had decided to marry him as second best.

"There was one other thing, Lydia."

"Yes?"

"I'm thinking of getting married again."

"Really?" She wanted to say something cutting about him really courting failure, but she refrained. "I hope you'll be happy this time," she said.

Jamie dipped his head in acknowledgement.

"She's a lovely person. She's been a social worker in Sheffield for nearly twenty years — not the easiest of jobs. Finally it just got on top of her and she had to get away. She has the village shop and post office in Kedgely."

My successor is a failed social worker and a postmistress, thought Lydia. All her old contempt returned. How pathetic Jamie always was! How small-scale his hopes and ambitions! And even in them he has failed. It humiliated her to think she had been married to him. It humiliated her to think of the sort of woman he was to marry next. It seemed to equate Lydia with her. And it would equate them in the minds of everyone in the district.

"And when will it take place, this marriage?" she asked.

"Oh, nothing's decided yet. Mary's been married before too, so she doesn't want to rush into it."

"You're just 'keeping company'?"

Lydia used the servant-girl expression with relish, but Jamie was unoffended. He smiled.

"That's pretty much it at the moment. Naturally we neither of us have a lot of spare time to spend with each other. But we're sort of feeling our way."

"How nice . . . but there was no need for you to tell me all this, you know. It's none of my business."

"And we're nothing to each other, as you said. Oh quite." Jamie got up. "Still these things are always a bit disconcerting when you hear them from strangers, aren't they? That's why I wanted to tell you myself."

"Yes, I suppose that's true," admitted Lydia.

"You've never thought of getting married again yourself?"

"No! Good heavens, no! I've had the fullest of lives without it. In fact, I'm always mystified by people — filmstars and suchlike — who get married over and over again. One *can* learn from experience, but it seems they never do."

If Jamie registered that this speech was intended to hold a message for him, he gave no sign. Lydia led the way out of the sitting room and to the front door. The interview, her stance implied, was over.

"And you've made a very satisfactory career for yourself, then, Lydia?" Jamie said, small-talking as he walked out of the house.

"Very satisfying, at any rate."

"And a nationally known name."

"Oh —" she gestured dismissively.

"But we did have happy times together as kids, Robert, you and I, didn't we?"

"We did. Goodbye, Jamie."

She shook his hand, watched him as he went out to the battered old Volkswagen, which no longer seemed such an amusing little car, only a symbol of his failures, and then shut the door without a wave of the hand.

She went back into the sitting room, and began to fix herself another drink. She rejected gin — somehow too maudlin a drink for her present mood — and poured herself a stiff whisky. Altogether a sturdier, more combative drink. Odd that Jamie should drink it now. Because he was one of nature's wimps, and a human disaster-area to boot. She added a little water to the glass and stood reflectively by the mantelpiece.

It did not please her that Jamie had come to live near her — did not please her at all. He was known in the area — they had spent their brief married life in a village not far from Bly, in a tiny house owned by her parents — and he had friends here, or had had. People would recognise him, and they would talk. She was one of the local notables: she was reviewed at length in the quality Sunday newspapers, and occasionally consented to be interviewed on radio or television. Hitherto she had been a writer with a brief marriage in her past. Now she was a woman with an ex-husband in the vicinity. It was not a change for the better, not a change that Lydia liked.

Because Jamie was not only a failure — he was one of *her* failures. He would be living and ever-present proof of the fallibility of her judgment — and in the most important decision of her life, as many people would see it. She had faced this fact within days of marrying him: when he had told her that his "job in the City" had been merely a "taking on trial" by a brokerage firm for a salary hardly more than nominal. He had shared with her his feeling that the trial had not been a success, and his judgment was confirmed within a fortnight. He was out of a job. As he was to be twice again in their brief marriage.

She had tried to give him backbone, perseverance, self-confidence. She had tried encouragement, exhortation, pushing, nagging. He had remained a well-disposed bumbler. If he's like this at twenty-four, she had thought with dread, what will he be like at fifty-five? "You'll never change him," Robert had said to her, the night before he left to trek across the Central Australian desert. "He accepts the things that happen to him, he never makes them happen. You'll have to take him as he is. He's nothing like me." The next evening she had told Jamie that their marriage had not been a success and she wanted him to move out. He had nodded and said she was probably right. Within a week he was gone, and for the next few years she had heard occasional pieces of news about him, mainly from his parents, whom he moved back with when he was down on his luck and out from when something turned up. For years she had heard nothing at all.

Suddenly she remembered that she had been momentarily reminded, even now, of Robert. And then something else occurred to her: Jamie's demeanour during their interview had not been at all what might have been expected. He had not been in the least apologetic or hangdog: there was nothing of the whipped cur, not in his carriage or his words. He had accepted his long log of failure with resigned dignity — even with amusement. When her words had been cutting he had registered them, but he had not been cut. He had not been in the least humble. He had smiled at her. Had he, even, smiled *at* her? Been, somehow, amused by her? Been showing tolerance of her and her ways? That was, somehow, what his style and stance had suggested. The idea was insupportable.

Especially when coupled with another one: that Jamie, belatedly and astonishingly, had been brought to normality and maturity by another woman. That a social-worker-cum-postmistress — a woman she would doubtless be kind to and despise in her heart — had done what she had never been able to do: had found things in Jamie which could be nurtured and strengthened, and by that loving care he had been saved. Was it that that gave Jamie that look when he gazed at her, that look of . . . amused tolerance?

Draining her glass she was suddenly seized by rage. She picked up the cushions on the sofa and flung them one by one at the wall, sending pictures askew, breaking a small ornament that fell from the sideboard. Then she seized those from the chairs and sent them flying at the windows, kicked the desk chair viciously and then took up her glass again and sent it to shatter against the solid oak door.

Then she ran sobbing with rage and frustration to her bedroom.

"Well, you did have a night last night," said Molly Kegan, Lydia's cleaning woman, when she saw the room the next morning. The two women smiled at each other. Lydia had not bothered to clean up. The two understood each other too well for that sort of subterfuge.

"A little release of tension," Lydia said.

"Book not going well?"

"Molly, when have you known me get worked up like that over a book?"

"Always a first time."

"I had a visit from my ex-husband last night."

The cleaning woman smiled and nodded.

"Oh well, there you are. Ex-husbands produce that kind of feeling. Husbands too, for that matter." Mrs Kegan was a divorced woman herself — unqualified, but much too intelligent for the charring work she was forced to undertake for her living. She had given herself to marriage and children, and now only the children remained. "What did he want — money?"

"Oh no — there was no question of my giving him money."

"Well, he surely didn't come just to talk over old times, did he?"

"No, he came to tell me that he has moved back to the area. He has a farm over near Kedgely. Organic, naturally: Jamie always was one for fads."

"And you don't want him anywhere near you?"

"Not in the least. Of all the farms in England he could have brought to bankruptcy, he has to choose one five miles from me!"

"Why did he, do you think? Spite? To harass you in some way or other?"

"I don't know. . . . There's a woman involved, but I don't know which came first, the woman or the farm."

"Ah well," said Molly Kegan, beginning to pick up the cushions. "What can't be cured must be endured."

"What a *spineless* proverb!" said Lydia. "I

bet if your husband came to live around here you'd do something."

"Apply for a court order," said Molly Kegan promptly. "There was physical violence, as you know. And there was mistreatment of the children. But you had nothing to complain of in that way, did you, Lydia?"

"Good Lord, no. All I had to complain of was that he was totally spineless and ineffectual. The original nowhere man."

"There you are. Nothing to complain of at all."

CHAPTER 6

"Stop yer bawling!" yelled Kelly Hoddle to the baby in the back seat. "We're going to Yorkshire whether you like it or not . . . And whether I like it or not."

The addition was said without rancour — a mere conversational gambit. Maurice Hoddle accepted it as such and grinned down at his wife.

"You know you'll enjoy showing off the baby," he said. "You'll get on fine when you're there."

"I always get on fine with people who accept me for what I am."

It was a matter-of-fact statement that was nothing less than the truth. Her husband looked at her with affection. The glorious not-quite-for-real blonde hair, the cheekily made-up face that gave her the look of a dissolute elf, the fine breasts and glorious legs that Kelly habitually flaunted with tight short skirts. Maurice felt a sudden spurt of lust that was incompatible with driving up the M1. He turned his eyes back to the road.

Kelly had hit the nail on the head as usual: people who could accept her as she was loved her — loved her sexually precocious gamine style, her unashamed Birmingham accent, her frank enjoyment of the physical and her uproarious love of all sorts of bad jokes. He had heard her laughter before he had seen her. It was at a casting session for *Waterloo Terrace,* and the moment he did see her he had known that she was right for the role, and right for him.

The role had been that of Sharon, the relief barmaid at the Dog and Whistle. So popular had been her cheekiness and the blatancy of her sexual aggression that the original three months' contract had been extended to two years. By then they were married, Kelly was pregnant, and was pronouncing the part "boring." She was always wanting to go on to something else — that was part of her appeal. But the parts, when they had come (and Maurice was in a position to make sure that they did come) had mostly been variations on Sharon the barmaid. Everyone had assumed that, like most actors in soaps, Kelly had taken a part that was not too far from her own personality. But though that was true of what might be called the basic Kelly, Maurice knew that she had many different sides to her personality, that she played from minute to minute many different roles. Though he would have admitted that she was never going to play

Cordelia or any of the three sisters he knew better than anyone that as yet she had not been fully stretched.

"I suppose you'll be going up to see that old cow," she said now. Maurice laughed, but his hands tightened on the steering-wheel and his voice, though it was chaffing in tone, did not hold real amusement.

"Now who could you mean by that? Lydia, conceivably? Yes — I'll go up and see her for old times' sake. My thick skin can take all the comments, spoken and unspoken, on the undignified and shoddy world of television."

"I'll be more interested to hear the comments on the common and sluttish nature of your wife. Because don't think I'll be going with you."

"On the whole it might be better if you didn't."

"Snooty old cow. Thinks her farts don't smell."

"You did rather overdo your act, the one time you met."

"Of course I did. Terribly well-bred people always give me the gips. . . . What part of my 'act' are you referring to, incidentally?"

"The 'born on the wrong side of the tracks' part."

Kelly gave a throaty laugh.

84

"That's no act."

"I've never actually heard your parents use a four-letter word. Nor do they keep their coal in the bath-tub, or live off National Assistance."

Kelly winked delightedly.

"I'll be overdoing my act again if she's unfortunate enough to encounter me in Bly. But I doubt if she will. She'll stick to her cottage — cottage! I'll bet it's no cottage! — the whole weekend. The spider at the centre of her web. Or that thing that devours her males. . . . I should hate her by rights."

Maurice's body was still tense, but he tried a careless laugh.

"Nonsense. I was never devoured."

"Of course you were. You had to . . . re-create yourself. I've talked to people who knew you when you started at Midlands Television. They say you were uncertain who you were, what you were doing, and had a gigantic inferiority complex about your brother."

Maurice's mouth crinkled with displeasure. Clearly this was news to him.

"Is that what they say about me? Lovely friends I have down there!"

"Good friends will tell the truth."

"If that's what they think about me, perhaps it is time I made a move."

"A move?"

She looked at him sharply. He drove on, more relaxed now they had got off the subject of his aunt.

"There have been some . . . feelers out, from Yorkshire Television."

"You've kept bloody quiet about them."

"I'm telling you now. . . . What do you think?"

"You haven't told me what the job is yet."

"Head of drama."

Kelly let out a whistle, then looked at him suspiciously.

"*Head* of drama? All drama? Not just the soaps? *Emmerdale* bleeding *Farm* and that sort of thing?"

"Head of drama. All drama . . . we could live in Leeds. We wouldn't necessarily want to live anywhere near Bly."

"Too bloody right we'll live in Leeds. I wouldn't want that woman to get her talons into you again."

"Don't get neurotic about Lydia. She's a figure in my past. From one point of view she's really rather pathetic."

Kelly, unusually, kept her counsel and occupied herself with putting the baby to rights in his carry-cot strapped to the back seat. But after a few minutes she did say:

"Or into Matthew either, when the time comes."

★ ★ ★

Two days earlier, on the Wednesday, the Bellingham boys had managed to get their mother along to the doctor's. Later, at tea time, they told Lydia about it.

"The doctor thinks she might have M.E.," said Ted. Lydia furrowed her brow.

"M.E? I think I've heard of it. I get confused by all these abbreviations. . . ."

"Myalgic encephalomyelitis. It means you get sort of listless and exhausted. Can't summon up the energy to do anything."

"You'd understand," said Colin, "if you'd seen us trying to get her to the doctor's this morning."

"Didn't she want to go?"

"I think she wanted to go," said Ted seriously. "I mean, she *really* wanted to see him. She just didn't want to *go*. Didn't want to make the journey. And surgery's only the other end of High Street. I thought I could get her there on my own, but in the end Colin had to stay away from school too."

"Pushing and shoving and half-carrying," said Colin, demonstrating. "And Mum weeping and saying we were cruel."

"It was awful," said Ted. "Everyone was watching. You know what Bly is like. But I thought if I just went along and asked the doctor to call they wouldn't believe it was as se-

87

rious as it is. I *knew* she was just sort of giving up."

"And is it serious, this M.E? Will she be ill for long?"

"Yes, she will. Maybe for years. It's very serious. Dr Cornish put her straight into hospital for tests."

"But how will you manage?"

"Oh, I expect we'll be all right," said Colin.

"Lots of hamburgers!" agreed Ted. "And pizzas. I love pizzas."

"But you can't get those in Bly."

"Dad can pick them up after work. And there's a marvellous fish and chip shop in North Radley. Colin and I can cycle there and pick it up."

"Don't any of you cook?"

"Dad can just about manage egg and bacon and sausage."

"And we can do hamburgers," said Colin. "Though it's easier just to pick them up at a McDonald's."

"I should hate to think of hamburgers looming as large as *that* in your diet," said Lydia. She felt she was bursting with happiness, but she suppressed her smile and adopted a businesslike manner. "What you must both do is come up here for a proper meal in the evening."

"No, it's all right," said Ted. "We *like* hamburgers and pizzas and things."

"That's neither here nor there," said Lydia briskly.

"It would be too much trouble," said Colin. "It would stop you working on your book."

"It would do nothing of the kind. I'm always finished work by four or five o'clock. Cooking for three is hardly more work than cooking for one, and it will be a great pleasure, which cooking for one hardly is. Will your father be home from work yet?"

The boys had gone to school in the afternoon and explained the situation to their headmaster. At a quarter to four they had cycled home to an empty house and then come straight up to Lydia. Ted looked at his watch.

"Not yet. About a quarter to six, probably."

"He knows the situation?"

"Oh yes. The doctor rang him. Mum was just crying and that, and a bit afraid, so the doctor did it. I spoke to him too and said we'd be all right."

"Well, I'll ring him a bit later on. Now, tonight may be a bit of a scratch affair —"

"No, really Mrs Perceval," said the boys. "We don't expect you to feed us without notice!"

"Deep freeze. No problem. Call me Lydia, by the way. So much easier. Now, the question is: what do you like *apart* from all that fast food junk?"

"Shepherd's pie!" said Ted. "With lots of tomato sauce!"

"Lasagne," said Colin.

"All that mince!" protested Lydia. "You must like something that isn't made with mince."

"Pork," said Colin, maturely considering. "I think pork's my favourite meat. Roast. Or pork chops."

"I quite like fish," said Ted. "And I know it's good for you, but I don't like it boiled or steamed. I like a good batter."

"And *chips*," said Colin. "Nice crispy ones, not ones from the packet you just put in the oven."

"That's when I *knew* Mum was ill," said Ted. "When she started serving instant chips."

Lydia felt blessed — somehow favoured. She felt as if some higher power had intervened. She noted down all their preferences in her head, and made mental notes of how she might lead them away from such basic forms of cuisine into something more interesting and inventive. It was going to give a new shape and purpose to her day. And it was going to last such a long time! Later on she rang their father.

"Mr Bellingham? This is Lydia Perceval.

90

The boys are up here, and they've been telling me about their mother. I really am most upset for you all. I hear it's a dreadful condition. . . . Yes, I'd gathered the treatment may take a long while. . . . Look, I've talked this over with Ted and Colin and I want to be responsible for giving them a proper meal each day. That would take a bit of the burden off you, wouldn't it? They can come up here after school — young people really shouldn't go home to an empty house, should they? — and I'll have a good hot meal for them in the evening."

"That's really very kind of you, but there's no n—"

"It's pure pleasure, I assure you, Mr Bellingham. It's good to know I can be of some little help. I'm rustling up something for them tonight, and they'll be back home by nine at the latest."

If it occurred to Lydia that it would be a kindness to include the boys' father in the invitation now and then, she suppressed the thought. Nick Bellingham had not sounded, from the boys' account of him, a man of any interest.

The Maple Tree had been a country pub from time pretty much immemorial, serving shepherds and dry-stone-wallers on a hilly

91

road ten miles from Halifax. Time and demographic changes had destroyed its custom, and five years before it had been taken over by a couple in flight from Chelsea, who had turned it into an up-market restaurant, all tarted up in an amusing way, and serving interesting and unusual food at interesting and unusual prices. Maurice had read about the place in the *Good Food Guide* (one of the legacies of Lydia's tutelage was that he liked his food, and liked to experiment with it, a taste he shared with Kelly). As soon as they arrived at Bly he insisted they were all going to the Maple Tree that night to celebrate his father having a job. Thea, conscious that she was a rather dull cook, rang around and fixed up a babysitter.

Just the sight of the prices made Andy uneasy, but what was the use of a son in television if you couldn't let him treat you to an expensive meal now and again? He swallowed his pride with his starter. It was while Kelly was still busy with a dish involving game pâté and prawns that someone from a nearby table — motherly, very Yorkshire, her body thickened by heavy food — came over to her with a piece of paper.

"Excuse me, but aren't you Sharon from *Waterloo Terrace*?"

Kelly turned a dazzling smile on the woman.

"That's right. Or rather I was."

Her accent was impeccably upper-middle: she might have been playing in *Private Lives*.

"It's funny but you don't sound a bit like her. But that's acting, isn't it? Do you think I could have your autograph for my daughter? She thought you were wonderful."

"Delighted. It's nice to be remembered."

She wrote "Best wishes, Kelly Marsh" on the piece of paper, gave one of her dazzling smiles, and returned to her prawny pâté in high good humour. Thea looked at her, fascinated.

"Are you always acting?"

"Most of the time, I suppose. . . . Except when I'm in bed."

"Ah."

"You can't act when you're asleep, can you? What did you think I meant?"

Kelly let out her barmaid laugh, conscious that by now the whole restaurant knew who she was.

"Kelly responds to whoever she's talking to," said Maurice, with a shy, wondering pride. "Like a chameleon. Only sometimes she makes herself more conspicuous against her background rather than camouflages herself."

"Like with your sister," said Kelly to Thea. "You don't mind me being rude about her, do you? No, I thought not. Put me up against an impeccably dressed middle-class female who I know is going to dislike me whatever I do and I become a slut. Or rather I exaggerate the slut in me, which is quite a lot of slut to start with. Where's my bleeding saddle of lamb? Service in this joint is pretty crumby, isn't it?"

Having made the lightning change back to barmaid Kelly settled down for a bit to watch the diners who were watching her.

"You'll go up and see Lydia over the weekend, will you, Maurice?" Thea asked.

"I'll pop up tomorrow. Get it over with."

"Ask her to lunch on Monday. She won't come, but it will be a gesture."

"You know she's got two new boys, do you?" Andy asked his son.

"New boys? What on earth do you mean? Toy boys?"

They all laughed.

"Even I wouldn't accuse Lydia of being the type who went in for toy boys. No, two lads from the village — they go to my school. She's . . . taking them over."

Maurice looked at his father with affection.

"Like she did me and Gavin, you mean? You shouldn't worry too much about that, you know. She just works on malleable adolescents. The effect doesn't last."

Thea saw Kelly raise her eyebrow slightly.

"You can't generalise, you know, Maurice," Andy said. "You may have got away, but that doesn't mean another boy will."

"Gavin —" began Thea, but then she shook her head vigorously. "No, we really shouldn't be talking about this on our first night out as a family for years, should we? When is this interview with Yorkshire Television, Maurice?"

"Monday afternoon. More of a meeting, really. Slightly clandestine. We'll pack up the car, Kelly and Matthew can look around Leeds for an hour or two, maybe talk to a few estate agents, then we'll be off down the M1 and home — out of your hair."

"You're not in our hair, Maurice," protested Thea, conscious that the more she saw of Kelly the more she was intrigued by her, even liked her.

"Oh, I know Dad has a lot to do with this new job."

"Last week of term next week," said Andy, shaking his head. "No problem — just a lot of loose ends to tie up."

He was conscious of a figure looming over their table. He thought at first it was another autograph hunter, but when he looked up it was Nick Bellingham, his paunch seeming ampler than when they had last met, his face certainly redder.

"Mr Hoddle? Don't let me interrupt. Just on my way out. Just thought I'd tell you we've found out what the trouble's been with the wife. Thought it was all in the mind m'self, but I was wrong. She's got M.E."

"Oh dear, I'm sorry. That's rather serious, isn't it?"

"So they tell me. May take months, years, before she's back to normal. But your sister-in-law's been very good. Offered to give the lads a good meal in the evenings, and she's been as good as her word. Load off my mind, I can tell you. I couldn't be more grateful — that's what I call being a Christian. Meant I could come out here tonight. She's a wonderful woman, that sister-in-law of yours. Goodnight all!"

And he lurched off towards the door. Back at the table there were now several pairs of raised eyebrows.

"Awful man," said Kelly.

Maurice sat looking thoughtful.

CHAPTER 7

On the Saturday afternoon Maurice took the old, familiar road up the hill to his aunt's cottage.

As he neared the brow he recalled his wife's sneer at the word "cottage." Of course she had hit the nail on the head as usual. There had been three labourers' cottages there in the old days: dark, cold little hovels. Lydia had removed doors, enlarged windows, made lawns, installed central heating, all with the proceeds of her first popular success, *Horatio and Emma*. It was now pre-eminently a gentlewoman's home, and the name Hilltop Cottage, a survival from its former lowly status, represented the sort of self-depreciation which Lydia would be the first to deplore in humans.

But there was no denying she had made it attractive. In the warm afternoon sun it glowed, as surely it never had glowed in its previous bleak existence. Maurice stood for a moment and looked at it: the terraced lawns and brilliant flower-beds framed it perfectly. This was Lydia's face to the world. He reflected that he was one of the very few people who knew her other face.

He went through the gate, carefully closing it after him. Then he walked down the path and up to the front door. Once he and Gavin had walked straight in and shouted greetings. Perhaps the new boys already did. He knocked.

"Maurice! How lovely to see you again! All alone?" Lydia could hardly keep the satisfaction from her voice. "Do come through. I've got the tea things ready."

She led the way through to the sitting room, then bustled into the kitchen to put the kettle on. She was wearing a stylish cream dress with a full skirt, perfect summer wear. Maurice stood leaning against the kitchen door — apparently relaxed, yet feeling a growing tension inside him, as if his entrails were being knotted.

"Yes, I'm on my own. Kelly is bathing Matthew, and Mother is helping her."

"Thea would love that. She always liked babies."

"I hope you'll like him too. Thea wondered whether you could come to lunch on Monday."

"Monday I'm in Boston Spa, I'm afraid. Research, you know. I always think babies have to do a lot of growing before they get interesting . . . But do thank Thea — so kind of

98

her. . . . I hope Matthew is a fine, healthy baby?"

"Oh, he is. Very forward for his age."

"Splendid. Now — cream biscuits? Though now I look at you, Maurice, you are a trifle overweight, aren't you?"

The irony crackled in her voice. Maurice looked down at his stomach.

"More than a trifle, Lydia. The *mot juste* would be 'decidedly'."

"Do you take enough exercise?"

"I'm not conscious of taking any."

"And I suppose you eat all the wrong foods?"

"Too much of the right ones, at any rate. You shouldn't be censorious on that score, Lydia. You taught me to enjoy good food, and as far as I'm concerned the only wrong food is bad food."

"I didn't teach you to eat immoderately, I hope! Right, well, let's go through, Maurice dear. Will you take the tray? That's right, on the little table here. How is the job going? Still writing for that — what's its name? — *Trafalgar Terrace*?"

Maurice didn't correct her. One of Lydia's little foibles was to make that sort of deliberate mistake about anything that she disapproved of.

"Yes, I still do a lot of writing for that.

It's still as popular as ever."

"I never see it. I never see anything much on the 'box'." She gestured towards a panelled part of the wall where, they both knew, a television set was concealed behind dark wooden doors. "News, now and then, and Parliament sometimes. But it's so strident. Standards of behaviour are not what they were."

"People have been saying that since the Reform Bill, as I'm sure you know, Lydia."

She gestured dismissively.

"Perhaps they're right. Perhaps it has been downhill all the way for a century and more. So, as I say, I see virtually nothing. But at least your wife — Kelly, such an odd name! I always think of the Isle of Man — at least Kelly has got out of *Trafalgar Terrace*. So perhaps you will too before long."

"*Waterloo Terrace* is something one aspires to get into, Lydia, not something one is desperate to get out of. And it's a programme that has its points. American soaps are all about money, but the English soaps are about community. The English ones do have a certain social value."

"What was it Dr Johnson said about disputing precedency between a flea and a louse?"

Maurice laughed, genuinely amused.

"That's very good, Lydia. You haven't lost

your touch. I don't suppose you'd change your opinion if I told you it was one of the most popular programmes on television?"

"Not in the least."

"I thought not. You don't change. Anyway, the good news is that I may have a new job in the future."

"Oh?"

"There's a possibility — no more — that I may become head of drama for Yorkshire Television."

Lydia raised her eyebrows rather quizzically as she poured two cups of tea and handed biscuits.

"Well, that certainly *sounds* rather grand. I was hoping you might get out of television, though."

"They're not queueing for my services at the National Theatre or the Royal Shakespeare Company."

"You should make them want you! Television is not at all what I hoped for you."

Maurice shook his head pityingly, feeling the knots inside him being tied more tightly.

"I'm sure it's not. But I rather think it's a mistake to hope for things from children."

"Nonsense. It's perfectly natural. And it gives them something to aim for."

"Well, I hope I accept Matthew for what

he is, and don't build up high expectations for him."

"Then he'll never come to anything. One builds up expectations based on what a boy *can be*. We all have it in us to be something, just as we all have it in us to fall back and be nothing. Sugar?"

"I'm afraid so."

Lydia was by now on a track she was unable to get off.

"If Gavin had lived he would have spurred you on to being something different."

Maurice looked down at his cup and saucer.

"Do you think so?"

"Of course he would. Gavin never gave in to weakness. Do you remember how afraid Gavin was of snakes?"

"I do."

"And yet we worked at it and freed him from fear, didn't we? Do you remember how we went over to the zoo at Manchester time and time again, getting him closer and closer, until eventually he was able to touch one of the snakes?"

"Yes, I do. I'm afraid that now I feel that was almost obscene."

Lydia grew pink with outrage.

"What nonsense! He conquered his fear!"

"He wasn't afraid because they were venomous."

"No — he just hated the texture of their skins. Quite irrational."

"I rather think that to the end of his life Gavin was afraid of snakes."

"You just want to think that because of your own failures of nerve."

Maurice sighed.

"I didn't come up here to quarrel, Lydia. I have many happy memories of being up here with Gavin."

"Of course." Lydia shook herself. "We've got off on the wrong foot somehow. Have another cup of tea. Cake?"

"Ah — the old seed cake. I'm impressed that you're still making it."

"Just started again. This is the first attempt, so I don't suppose my hand is in yet. I've got — there are some boys — boys I'm helping to look after. Their mother is in hospital — something rather serious with an abbreviation I've forgotten."

"M.E. Its full name is myalgic encephalomyelitis. Midlands did a programme about it."

Lydia looked at him sharply.

"You know the boys?"

"No, their father came up to us while we were eating at the Maple Tree last night," said Maurice, feeling obscurely that he had scored a point. "He seemed rather dim."

Lydia nodded, contentedly.

"That's the impression I've got from the boys. And the mother is a nonentity. Still, that can be . . . made up for. They're very bright boys."

As if on cue the front door was opened and the boys burst in. They pulled themselves up short when they saw that Lydia had a visitor and stood in the doorway shyly.

"Sorry," said Ted. "Didn't realize —"

"You must be the nephew in television," said Colin. "Married to Sharon the barmaid."

"That's right," said Lydia, getting up and doing the hostessly thing. "This is my nephew Maurice. Colin, Ted."

"How do you get into television?" asked Ted.

"All sorts of ways," Maurice said, having been asked the question all too often before. "Local journalism, local radio. There are quite a few courses run by colleges and polytechnics."

"I expect it would suit Colin better than me," said Ted regretfully. "You'd have to be really bright, wouldn't you? Outgoing and super-intelligent?"

"I would have thought super-intelligent people were just the sort television companies would be unable to find a use for," said Lydia tartly. Maurice shot her a look. She really knew how to twist the knife. But then he sat back in his chair and laughed.

104

"Actually there are all sorts in television, including rather dull ones like me. Sometimes you look at your colleagues and say 'How on earth did he get a job in the industry?' But you look at others and say 'Why on earth is he wasting his time here?' The truth is, I think, that you'd find the same in any other job. Life is one big accident."

"Nonsense, one *makes* one's life," said Lydia.

The elder boy seemed to sense a tension.

"We're off to the gravel pit," he said. "We'll be an hour or two. Is that all right?"

"Of course," said Lydia, smiling at them fondly. "I'll have your dinner ready around six thirty."

The boys gave a wave of the hand and charged out. Already they were treating Lydia's cottage as home, Maurice noted. It had happened more slowly with Gavin and him. But then the parental situation had been very different with them, and Lydia had had to move more delicately. Here it seemed as though she was moving in to fill a vacuum. And of course now she had had practice.

I am not going to let Lydia work me up again, Maurice told himself.

"They seem nice lads," he said neutrally, concentrating on finishing his cake.

"They are, and very bright. Colin especially."

"The younger in this case."

"Yes. The younger this time."

"You must be careful with Ted, then."

Lydia smiled a regal but steely smile.

"Oh Maurice, of *course* I will."

"He seems to have the notion already that he's more ordinary than his brother."

"Ted has sterling qualities — good, sturdy, old-fashioned ones. I'm sure they'll make his way for him. As you say, their home background is pretty impoverished, intellectually speaking. Coming here is an education for them both."

"E-ducare, to draw out," said Maurice, smiling as he quoted her.

"Precisely. You remember."

"Have you any plans for them?" he asked cunningly.

"I'll get to know them a lot better before I have plans. Colin will be much easier than Ted." She did not notice an infinitesimal and sad shake of the head from Maurice. "I think I shall leave them both a little bit of money. Not a lot — I don't believe in people having it easy. But enough to provide an initial fillip, should I not be around. The bulk, as you know, goes to Robert."

"Of course. You know you don't have to explain. Kelly and I have more than enough for our needs. . . . You've always liked adventurous people, haven't you, Lydia?"

"Yes, I have. I make no apology for that. 'Safety First' has always seemed a contemptible rule to live one's life by. Robert will *use* the money, not just have it. Some expedition somewhere — several, probably. I've never remotely lived up to my income. But I think the boys should have a few thousand each, to get their lives off to a good start."

Maurice shifted in his chair, conscious that his resolution not to get worked up was going by the board.

"Don't cut the parents out, will you, Lydia?"

"Of course not. But the mother seems to have cut herself out for the time being."

"She hasn't cut herself out — she's *ill*. M.E. is a very nasty illness. She'll need all the love and affection and attention she can get from her family."

"Of course. I've told them they should go to the hospital tomorrow. This will be an anxious time for her — with all the tests and uncertainty. Ted in particular is very affectionate, very protective. Colin seems to be more open — more inclined to welcome new experiences."

"Don't make distinctions between them, Lydia."

She pursed her lips in irritation.

"You are in a lecturing mood today, Maurice. One has to make distinctions between people because people are different. So naturally one plans different things for them."

"E-ducare — to draw out," said Maurice.

"I don't *impose* my plans on people!" said Lydia sharply. "God knows, you yourself are proof of that. You and Gavin were always perfectly free to do what you wanted."

"Perhaps. But we all knew that Gavin was doing what pleased you, and I was doing what didn't please you."

"That was your prerogative, your freedom."

"Perhaps I would have done the sort of thing you planned for me if I hadn't always had this sense that you regarded me as so clearly the inferior of the two."

"Nonsense!"

"Not nonsense at all. The feeling was always present."

Lydia's mouth curled.

"Are you sure it was *me* that gave you that feeling?"

"Yes. Because it was with you that I always felt it. If Gavin and I were alone I never did."

"Gavin was so good."

Maurice was engulfed by a cold rage.

"You mean it was good of Gavin not to make

me feel my inferiority every minute of the day, don't you? Perhaps you're right. Gavin was good. He was a lot of other things besides: ruthless, muddled, idealistic, cold. . . ."

"I *know*. Do you think I didn't know Gavin through and through?"

Maurice got up and looked down at her.

"No. No, I don't think you did. There were a lot of sides to him, lots of things he thought and felt, that you never knew about."

Lydia's rage was open, and showed in her face.

"I knew Gavin through and through. I knew Gavin as no one else could because only I could really understand him, only I could appreciate his qualities."

"You couldn't know him as a brother could."

"Nonsense."

"And you couldn't understand him either, not deep down, because you always saw him in an idealistic glow, surrounded by a haze of heroism."

"Gavin had greatness in him."

"And because he knew you thought that he hid so much from you."

"He did not!"

"You knew he was terrified of snakes. You never knew the other thing that terrified him."

"What do you mean? What other thing?"

They were standing by the door, tense, angry. Maurice looked her straight in the eye.

"Gavin was terrified of fire."

Lydia's face crumpled with pain as she remembered his end. She let out a sob as Maurice turned and marched down the hallway and through the front door to the light.

It was impossible to settle to anything after Maurice had gone. Lydia dried her eyes quickly, put determinedly from her mind that terrible picture of the ball of fire on the *Sir Galahad*. But all she could think of to do was start some preparations for dinner. She peeled and sliced potatoes, arranged them in a casserole with milk, and put them in the oven. Then she put pork chops under the grill, to be turned on when the boys came in. All the time her mind was working furiously, organising the details of the scene she had just gone through.

He had been jealous of Gavin all his life — that much was obvious: jealous of his greater promise, jealous of the greater interest she took in him. It must have festered, as the meaner sorts of feeling generally did. There were moments in their argument when it had seemed as if he hated her.

Perhaps it wasn't just jealousy festering:

110

perhaps Thea had got at him — Thea and Andy. Well, they were welcome to have back the one who was not worth getting. Maurice would never amount to anything: if he were ever to conceive any ambition worth having, that foul-mouthed slut he had married would kill it stone dead.

It would be different with Colin and Ted.

The thought of them cleared her mind miraculously. She was a woman who hated stewing over problems, hated the eternal tramping through emotional marshlands which she saw as the disease of the twentieth century. One thing she had decided on was to do something for the boys financially. That at least she could do now. She went into the study, took down the phone book and found the home number of her solicitor in Halifax.

"Oliver? It's Lydia Perceval . . . Fine — no, no problems. It's just that when I make a decision I like to act on it at once. Now, I want a codicil to be added to my will — I think it can be done in a codicil. Have you got a pen handy? I want the sum of three thousand pounds each — no, make that five — to go to Colin and Edward Bellingham — spelt as you would expect. . . Yes, of *course* there's plenty of money to cover it. You know that, Oliver. It will hardly affect Robert's inheritance at all. I'll call in late on Monday to sign it on my way back from Boston Spa. Right?"

She had turned her back to the open window, so she had not seen the figures of the boys on their way round to the back door.

CHAPTER 8

On Monday morning Lydia had a quick breakfast of tea and toast, then piled books and
notepads into the back of her Saab. The garage
was at the back of her cottage, tidily tucked
away, and after locking up the cottage Lydia
drove down the bumpy lane that skirted her
back garden and on to the road. She felt light
of heart. Quite apart from the change in her
personal life, she enjoyed doing the sort of
research that lay ahead of her that day. She
was thorough yet efficient, knowing exactly
the sort of thing that she wanted, and where
to go for it. Her man was now king and (however unwisely he would use his power) she
enjoyed dealing with people who controlled
their own destiny, and a nation's.

Lydia used her car very infrequently, but
she was a perfectly confident driver, subject
only to occasional lapses in concentration
when her own affairs or those of her subject
of the moment took over and dominated her
mind. She negotiated the early morning traffic
and got to Boston Spa without mishap. Once
in the Library she collected from the desk the
books and documents which Dorothy Eccles

had ordered for her, and settled down at a desk in the small readers' area. She worked solidly for an hour, pausing only to give a wave of recognition to Dorothy when she passed. Dorothy was in her fifties, grey-haired and mousey in dress and demeanour. Her musty brown skirt and jumper and her heavy, low-heeled shoes affected Lydia adversely, as did her way of looking at her, devotedly. "If I were that kind of person," she had once said to herself, "I could enjoy being cruel to Dorothy." That was when she had decided to be conspicuously kind. Today Dorothy kept tactfully in the background, and it was only when Lydia got up to consult Larousse about an unfamiliar word that Dorothy came over to her apologetically.

"You did say around twelve, didn't you, Lydia?"

"Around twelve?"

"For lunch. Of course if it's not convenient —"

Lydia wiped a blank look from her face immediately.

"Oh — forgive me, Dorothy. I'm back in 1825. Yes, of course. We said we'd go to La Tavola Calda, didn't we? Do you think you could ring them? Order a table for twelve fifteen, and say I'll have veal milanese, and then whatever you would like. It will save a lot of hanging around. Will you come along at twelve and *haul* me back to the nineteen-nineties?"

She smiled her warmest smile. Lydia was not a warm person, but she had a warm smile for people like Dorothy Eccles, and it seldom failed to charm them. Dorothy smiled, devotedly, and Lydia bent back over her Larousse.

Promptly at twelve Dorothy padded along on her sensible shoes and dragged Lydia from the reactionary excesses of Charles X and Villèle. They drove in Lydia's car and talked all the way about the French Restoration. Dorothy knew enough — had recently taught herself enough — to be an excellent sounding-board. At La Tavola Calda they ordered a glass of wine each, and were soon tucking into veal milanese and Venetian liver, fussed over by a pair of waiters who knew Lydia was a "name," and so refrained from treating them with the sort of contempt they usually kept for middle-aged ladies on their own.

"So it's going well is it, the book?" Dorothy asked.

"Very well. No problems on the horizon that I can see. I could well have it finished by Christmas."

"Did you see what the Huddersfield Choral Society are doing next week?"

"No. You know I never notice such things, Dorothy."

"Cherubini's 'Mass for the Coronation of Charles X'."

"Really?"

"Yes — isn't it a coincidence? I wondered if you'd like to come along. I have two tickets."

Lydia stopped eating and considered.

"It would be interesting, though you know I have no ear for music. I could add a paragraph to my chapter on the coronation, which isn't in final form yet. . . . But no — I think you'll have to report on it for me, Dorothy. You see — I have . . . well, I have responsibilities in the evenings now."

"Responsibilities?"

Dorothy's face was curious, but rather as if she expected to hear that Lydia had been adopted by a stray cat or dog.

"Yes, it's fallen out most . . . oddly." She had nearly said "luckily," but her quarrel with Maurice on Saturday had made her more careful about words. "There are these two boys — awfully promising lads — and we've been getting to know each other: you know, chatting when they go past on their bikes, that sort of thing. And they've been up to tea."

"They're sort of . . . protégés?"

"Well, in a way, but they're *friends* mainly.

I've always had a bit of a gift for getting on with young people."

"I'm sure you have, Lydia."

Dorothy was gazing at her in her most cow-like fashion, and Lydia had to repress a spasm of irritation.

"Anyway, they've mentioned their mother, who sounded a bit of a cipher, frankly, but now it turns out that she's *ill* — got something called M.E. Likely to be out of the w— out of commission for months, as far as I can make out."

"Yes, it's a very slow condition to cure. There's quite a literature about it, you know, published in the last few years."

"What's its full name again?"

"Myalgic encephalomyelitis."

"That's it. Could you rustle up one or two of the books, do you think? Or take some photocopies? I could do with something really informative about it — I could calm the boys' fears. Anyway, the mother is in hospital, for tests first, then treatment, and that's left the father in charge. He sounds — I hope I'm not doing him an injustice — a bit of an oaf. Not at all the sort of man to do anything positive for the boys."

"So you've taken over, have you, Lydia?"

"Well, not exactly *that*, but I phoned him and said I'd take responsibility for the boys in the evenings: see that they get one really good meal a day, and so on."

"That's awfully good of you. And it will give you an interest."

"I hardly need an interest, Dorothy."

"No, I mean a *personal* interest: people. . . ."

Dorothy felt she had made a blunder. Lydia left a pause.

"Anyway, it means I'm cooking a lot more, making pies and custards and cakes, getting back all the old skills I've let fall into disuse since my nephews . . . grew up."

"Oh yes. You told me how fond you used to be of your nephews. How old are these boys?"

Lydia somehow didn't like the way she said "these boys," as if they were replacements ordered from Harrods.

"Colin and Ted? Colin is thirteen, Ted fifteen."

"Oh, so old. I thought you meant younger children."

"Oh no. The early teens are just the age I find most interesting. There is so much possibility and promise there."

"I'm sure you'll bring it out." Dorothy said it very sincerely, but she was conscious she had made bloomers she had to atone for. "What plans do you have for them?"

"No plans at all, beyond what to give them for tonight's dinner. To have plans is to invite disappointment. I shall watch and see how they develop. Oh — I do plan to leave them a little money. I'm stopping off at my solicitor's in Halifax on the way home. Goodness, look at the time. We must rush. I've acres of things to get through and I really must finish by four fifteen. Heavens, what *shall* I give them for their dinner?"

"There's a good butcher two or three doors down from here."

"Is there? Dotty, you are a treasure! What would I do without you?"

She settled the bill, brushing aside Dorothy's attempts to pay her share, and they picked up a couple of rump steaks before getting in Lydia's car.

"I'll just have scrambled eggs," said Lydia. "Two proper meals a day is too much for me. I think I'll do chips for them. Children do love chips, don't they? I'll try to teach them about good food, but I'll do it slowly. Looking at Maurice I wonder whether I should do it at all."

"Is that the one in television?"

"That's right — Gavin's brother. He called over the weekend. He was up visiting Thea. He is most definitely overweight. A man of thirty-odd should *not* be that shape."

119

"How nice that he keeps in touch."

"Hmmm. He's married to the most appalling woman. An actress, for want of a better word. The sort of woman who uses four-letter words in public. I'm afraid Maurice is never going to come to anything."

"What a disappointment for you."

Lydia nodded and drove on. When they got back to the library she said "To work, to work!", waved briefly to Dorothy and settled down at her desk. So absorbed did she become in the clericals and anti-clericals, going off on to an enticing by-way concerning Stendahl, that it was after half past four when Dorothy leaned over her shoulder and said:

"I thought you were aiming to be off by a quarter past, Lydia."

"Oh, my God! Why didn't you — ? Sorry, not your fault at all, Dorothy. Look, can this and this and this be kept for me for another week or ten days?"

"Of course."

"You're a treasure. I must fly."

By the time Lydia had got to her car she had decided to give her solicitor a miss: she could go in at any time and sign the codicil. Much better to be home by the time she had told the boys she would be in. But when she got back to the cottage she found a note from Molly Kegan saying the boys had rung during their lunch-break to say they were going swimming after school, and wouldn't be back at the cottage before six.

Lydia was pleased they showed such signs of responsibility. She peeled potatoes and cut them up into chips, then got the grill ready for the steaks. She cracked eggs into a saucepan and added cream and butter, and put a slice of bread under the grill.

The boys were boisterous and happy when they arrived. They had enjoyed their swim and were now ravenously hungry.

"Steak and chips — super!" said Ted.

"How do you like your steak done?" asked Lydia.

"Properly done," said Colin.

"Not red — yuck!" said Ted.

"In France," said Lydia, when they were all sat down and eating, "they would just give the steak a quick burst of heat on both sides, and that would be it."

"Well, that's France," said Ted. "Just because the French do it one way doesn't mean it's the best, does it?"

"The French know an awful lot about cooking."

"I think you should have food as you like it," said Colin, "not as someone else thinks you ought to like it."

"And if you're a natural vegetarian," said

Ted, "I mean, if you'd *like* to be a vegetarian, and think that killing animals for food is pretty nasty when you come to think about it, only you can't be one because most vegetables are so yucky, then you wouldn't want to eat your meat red, would you? I mean, you cut into it and it sits there saying: 'Flesh'."

"Shut up, you nerd," said Colin, brandishing his knife. "You're putting me off."

"Well, I hope you'll put off being a vegetarian until your mother is better," said Lydia. "I really wouldn't know what to cook for you. I'm an unrepentant meat-eater myself, *and* I have a fur coat — call me a wicked woman if you will."

After dinner Ted rang the hospital to say they wouldn't be going in that evening.

"Did you say you would?" asked Lydia.

"Well, we did, but the swimming really tired us out. I've said we'll be in tomorrow, *definitely*."

"She barely recognises us, you know," said Colin.

"Or we hardly know *her*," said Ted, clearly very troubled.

"It's like talking to someone who is *almost* someone you know."

"Eerie," said Colin.

Then they played Monopoly, which was Colin's favourite game. Lydia had given her

122

set away when the Hoddle boys grew up, but the Bellinghams had brought theirs up two nights before, and had left it with her. They're settling in, Lydia had thought.

Lydia played well, and played to win. She had no patience with people who pandered to children and let them win. The boys were more haywire in their approach, but Colin had a run of luck and finally drove Lydia to the wall.

"Perhaps I'll become a great capitalist," he said.

It was twilight, and time for them to leave.

"Thanks for a super meal," said Ted.

"My pleasure. Will your father be in?"

"Oh yes. He's got a lot of paperwork to go over for the firm. He was going to have bacon and eggs and get stuck into it."

"I think I'll walk down the hill and say hello to him. It's such a lovely evening, and we really ought at least to recognise each other if we pass in the street."

So the boys collected up their things, including a little pile of homework they had managed to forget about, and all three left the cottage, Lydia locking up behind her. It was indeed a lovely evening, with birds singing in the gathering darkness, and the air still warm. The boys collected their bicycles from beside the gate and wheeled them down the hill, the three of them talking animatedly. When they got to the bottom and the little collection of houses, shops and pub that constituted Bly, they turned right.

"I'll find out which your house is too," said Lydia. "I think I know which it is, but now I'll be sure."

They went past Andy and Thea's house, that regrettable mixture of stone on the ground floor and half-hearted timbering on the first. There was a dusty Volvo parked outside.

"I think that must be Maurice's," said Lydia, peering at it in the gloom. "I thought he said he'd be gone by now."

"It's a Midlands number plate," said Ted.

"Something must have kept him," said Lydia, speeding up a little. "Andy and Thea will be pleased."

"Andy Hoddle," said Colin. "Isn't it an awful name?"

"It doesn't have any ring to it," agreed Lydia.

"He's a good teacher, though," said Ted.

"I'm glad to hear it. Though I never could take science seriously somehow."

The house Nick Bellingham had bought when the family moved North was even more regrettable than the Hoddles'. It was a mean, four-square brick construction, with a skimpy apron of garden in the front, and a larger stretch of wilderness at the back. Lydia, in fact, could remember the house being built, and how she had thought it disfigured the village. The boys barged in through the front door and shouted to their father.

"Dad! Mrs Perceval's here."

Nick Bellingham had obviously been doing his paperwork in a state of comfortable dishabille. His shirt was open to his paunch, and he was struggling with his belt. His fly was just about done up, but it looked like a near thing. He was in his stockinged feet, and wildly looking round for somewhere to stub out his cigarette. He looked, in fact, a mess.

"Oh, Mrs Perceval. I wasn't expecting you. You must excuse the mess —"

Lydia was gracious.

"I won't notice it, because I won't come in. I thought it was such a lovely evening that I'd just come down with the boys and make myself known to you."

Nick was still feverishly buttoning himself up.

"Well, it's a great pleasure — and I want you to know I appreciate what you're doing — we all do —"

Lydia waved his gratitude aside.

"It's pleasure on *my* part, I assure you, Mr Bellingham."

"They've been good, I hope."

"Oh *Dad!* —"

"Of course they have. You've two very promising boys there. Now I won't disturb you any more, and I must be off home."

And smiling goodbye to the boys Lydia wafted out, leaving Nick Bellingham with the vague feeling of having been visited by royalty.

Lydia walked back through the village, rather pleased than otherwise that her image of the Bellingham father as pretty louche and unsatisfactory had been so thoroughly confirmed. She walked quickly past the Hoddle house, in case anyone should come out and she be asked in. The last person she ever wanted to meet again socially was that disastrous wife of Maurice's. She turned up the hill, where street-lighting soon stopped. The way was so well known that she went without hesitation. She had left lights on in the cottage, so it stood gleaming at the top of the hill, a beacon. Lydia felt very happy — at peace with herself and with life.

As she let herself in by the gate she thought: it's years since I've been so happy, so hopeful. She took the key from her pocket and let herself in the front door. Coffee, she wondered? No, perhaps a cup of drinking chocolate. She went into the kitchen and put a saucepan of milk on the hot-plate.

Then she remembered her missed appointment of the afternoon. Really it would be only courteous to ring Oliver Marwick at home and apologise. And make an appointment for Tuesday or Wednesday, because she wanted to get the thing done. She walked through to the study, picked up the phone, and dialled.

"Oliver? I *do* apologise for this afternoon. I was over in the library at Boston Spa and I got so immersed in things I didn't notice the time. The book's at a very interesting stage . . . You're sure? I do hate failing to keep appointments. Now when can I — ?"

She was disturbed by a tiny noise. She turned her head, startled.

"What's that? But — Rob — ?"

That was the last Oliver Marwick heard. The line went dead, and thinking that Lydia had had an unexpected visitor he went back to watching television.

CHAPTER 9

The news was brought down to Bly by a farmer's wife who had been hailed down by a distraught Molly Kegan at Lydia's gate.

"She's been murdered!" she kept saying. "I can't go back in there. And they say you mustn't touch anything."

Molly had stayed at the cottage gate and the farmer's wife, on her way into Halifax, had stopped at the post office in Bly and rung the police from there. The news had caused a great sensation among the two old people who were collecting their pensions and the postmistress, who saw her function as keeping the community alive by spreading any piece of information or misinformation that came her way. Within half an hour most people in the village had heard.

The news stunned them, though there was no sorrow. There was a time when Thea and Lydia had both been popular in Bly — when Thea was a young mother, Lydia a divorcée, and the sisters always in and out of each other's homes. Thea was still regarded with respect and affection, though there was also a sort of reserve on account of her great grief. Lydia, on the other hand, had become merely an occasional sight in Bly, and her dealings with the Hoddle boys in the past was a matter of general censure. The feeling towards her was little more than a vague feeling of pride that she was local and had made a name for herself in the world. She had been the most notable person in the area, and now she was a notable corpse.

"So, who is she — was she?" asked Charlie Peace of his superior as the police car from the West Yorkshire police headquarters in Leeds sped towards Bly.

Mike Oddie frowned.

"I ought to know more than I do, because I know the name. I wish I'd had time to ask my wife. Some kind of popular historian — biographer I think. People like Nelson, Lawrence of Arabia. There's always a good solid market for biographies of the right sort, as I understand it. But she was very scholarly — not the gush and grovel kind. I know Margaret has read one or two of her books — they sell well in paperback."

"So fairly prosperous?"

Mike shrugged.

"Depends what sort of a spender she was, I suppose."

"And she was strangled?"

"So I understand from the Halifax people."

"Someone with a fair degree of strength, then."

"Depending on whether she was awake or asleep, whether it was the culmination of a quarrel or she was caught by surprise. You're jumping the gun, Charlie. You could be making all sorts of assumptions that will have to be revised when you get to the scene of the crime. That way trouble lies, especially if you're the sort of person who doesn't easily revise your ideas. Much better to get to the scene with your mind a blank sheet."

"OK — mind a perfect blank."

Charlie grinned at the Superintendent equably. Oddie had noticed him soon after he had arrived in Leeds. He was chatting with a group in the police canteen, apparently relaxed, but Oddie could see from his eyes that he was registering everything said, noting who was the thickie and who was the bright boy, who the rebel and who the greaser. Now he was sitting sprawled in the car as if his limbs were dough, but Mike knew he was registering everything, and keeping it filed.

"How is Yorkshire treating you so far?" he asked.

"Pretty well. I'm really liking it. Only problem is understanding the natives."

"They probably have the same problem with you."

"No they don't. They all watch *East-Enders*."

Charlie — Dexter to the registrar of his birth — Peace had transferred to the detective squad of the West Yorkshire Police only two months before. He still spoke, and probably always would, broad cockney.

"Why did you decide to transfer up here?"

"Girlfriend. Got a girlfriend lives in Wakefield."

"Going to be married?"

"Oh, I don't know that we'll go *that* far."

They both laughed.

"No problems with her parents?"

Charlie grimaced.

"No. They're so liberal it's almost depressing."

"Nothing to get your teeth into?"

"That's about it. I rather enjoy a bit of a barney." Charlie gave one of his ferocious grins, but then he shifted in his seat. "When I said I applied for a transfer because of my girlfriend that wasn't quite true. We're fairly steady, but not *that* steady."

"Why did you then?"

"I was born in London, brought up there. I've been on the windy side of the law once or twice myself, and I know a lot of people who are well on that side. I just know too much, know what I mean? Coming North was like coming to a foreign country."

"The blank sheet of paper again."

"That's right."

"And is it? A foreign country, I mean."

"Yes," said Charlie emphatically. "And people down South think of it like that. You know, I once had a girlfriend whose parents *really* cut up rough on the race thing, and she said: 'You shouldn't let it worry you. When I had a boyfriend from Bolton, all they could say was: "But he's from the *North!*"' I never could work out whether that should make me feel better or worse."

They laughed, and drove on in companionable silence for the rest of the way.

When they came to Bly, Mike Oddie said: "It's through the village and up the hill, so the Halifax people tell me." They went past a few houses and the odd depressed-looking shop, past The Wheatsheaf, and then saw a hilly road to their left. There was a little knot of police and other cars at the top. Charlie turned up the hill, then left the car with the others. The two men got out and stood looking at the cottage, shimmering in the sun.

"Nice," said Charlie appreciatively.

"Exactly — that answers your question about whether she had money," said Oddie.

"I meant nice aesthetically," said Charlie, from the height of his six O levels and one A.

"Nice aesthetically costs money. You need brass to live in a place like this. Come on."

In the cottage the hive of activity that always succeeds a murder was beginning to scale down. The police surgeon, whom Oddie knew well, was snapping the clasps of his bag shut and getting to his feet.

"Morning, Mike," he said, raising his hand in greeting. "I'll get the initial report to you as soon as I can. No great surprises beyond what you can see for yourself, so far as I can say at this time. Time of death — somewhere between eight thirty and midnight. Unofficially I'd say you could lop off an hour either side of that, just as a working hypothesis, but that's unofficial."

He edged his way out of the working melee, gave another wave of the hand, and was off, leaving Mike and Charlie with an unobstructed view of the body.

"Oh," said Charlie.

"Take it slowly," advised Oddie. "Look away, keep calm, and then look back again."

Charlie looked at the ceiling, holding his heaving stomach. He took another peek, looked away, then contemplated the awful thing full on. Lydia was indeed a horrible sight, the elegant legs and cream-frocked body ending in the livid horror of her face, and the hideous, thin, discoloured line around her neck.

"She's by the phone," said the inspector from Halifax, coming up behind them and shaking hands with Oddie. He seemed to be relieved at handing the case over. "We think that may have been how she was surprised. She seems perfectly fit, but there was no great evidence of struggle — just some strands of rope under her fingernails, which luckily were fairly long. The phone was put back — he even seems to have turned off a saucepan of milk in the kitchen."

"Tidy murderer."

"There's a pane missing in one of the sitting-room windows, and some dirt on the sill. Doesn't look awfully convincing to me."

"You think he came through the door?"

"That would be my bet. Either it wasn't locked, or he had a key — probably the latter, since he tried to fake a break-in. But you'll make up your own minds about that. We'll be finished in twenty minutes or so, then we'll do some routine things that we can do in the village or from HQ: see if we can chase up any relatives, see if anyone was seen around last night. Ah — they're coming for the body now."

When the men with the stretcher had removed the livid remains of the elegant body that had been Lydia Perceval, and when the technical men from Halifax had packed up their little boxes and their cameras, Mike Oddie looked at Charlie.

"Blank sheet," he said. "Let's go round and see what impressions we get. Ask if there's anything that puzzles you."

So they went their separate ways around the study, then into the living room, the kitchen, and upstairs to the unrevealing bedrooms. It was, perhaps not surprisingly, the room where they had started, the study, that told them most.

"Charles the tenth," said Charlie, bending over a pile of typescript on a table beside the desk. "Our Charles will be the third when his time comes. Who's Charles the tenth?"

Mike came over and looked at the early pages.

"'The last king of France,'" he read out.

"I thought that was Louis the sixteenth," said Charlie, with a vivid downward chop of the hand.

"No, there was a restoration after Napoleon," said Mike. He read on. "Then another revolution in 1830, followed by Louis Philippe, who called himself King of the French, not of France."

"So now I know," said Charlie.

He went over to the bookcase set on its own under the window, full of volumes in pristine condition.

"Her books," he said. *Horatio and Emma* — that's Nelson and Lady Whatsit, isn't it? *Richelieu, Richard II, Lawrence of Arabia* — wouldn't you need Arabic to write that?"

"I think an awful lot of people have managed without," said Oddie.

"Byron, Frederick the Great — talented lady."

"Yes, they're a varied bunch. And look at all those paperback editions — American ones too. And translations. Looks like she must have made a packet."

Charlie turned away from the stuffed-full bookcase and peered at a framed photograph on the wall.

"Who are Tweedledum and Tweedledee?" he asked.

"Oh, I've seen that photograph before," said Oddie, coming up behind him. "It's very well known. It's George V and the last Tsar of Russia, Nicholas the whatever."

The two gazed gravely at the camera, the modest and successful constitutional monarch, the disastrous autocrat. The lower part of both their faces was covered by thick but neat beards. It was impossible to tell them apart.

"Like as two peas," said Charlie.

"There was a book of hers you missed out on," said Oddie. "*The Girlhood of the Last Tsarina*. A slim volume — looked older than the rest. Maybe her first go."

"Russian too? She must have been a marvellous linguist."

"No, the last Tsarina was a German princess, that I do know. She became more Russian than the Russians, but it counted against her in the First World War. Lydia Perceval probably had French and German, like most people of her generation. She'd have had to manage medieval French, though, to write some of those books."

"Later on she went for men, didn't she? I mean to write books on. Particularly strong, magnetic men."

"Ye-e-es. That does roughly seem to be the pattern, though I suspect also subjects whom she thought people might get interested in, who had had no biography of themselves written in English. Well, what general impressions have you got?"

"General?" Charlie sat himself down, sprawling, in a chair and thought. "A dominating sort of person, though perhaps subtle about it. She commands her space rather than just lives in it. It's a *distinguished* house, but it has no cosy, lived-in feel to it: everything has its place, everything in its place."

"Except perhaps here," Oddie pointed out.

"Yes — the study seems the centre of the house, and here the research has taken over, making a bit of a mess, though no more than you might expect — it's ordered mess, really."

"Anything else?"

"Conservative with a small c. Probably with a large C too, with her admiration of strong men. Writes in longhand, beautifully clear, then types it up. All the china was traditional in design, all the ornaments in good, old-fashioned taste. Curtains and furnishings good quality but far from modern. A spinster's home, wouldn't you say? A very self-sufficient person."

"Yes — and some of the guest bedrooms didn't feel as if they'd been used in years. But there was that picture of two boys."

"That was ages old," Charlie pointed out. "Boys don't dress like that these days."

"One of them is this naval chap." Oddie pointed to the photograph on the bookcase. Charlie got out of his seat and strolled over to look at it again.

"Doesn't he think he's the cat's whiskers!" he said derisively.

"Hmmm. Doesn't look entirely comfortable to me. There's an element of play-acting or perhaps bravado there. You haven't mentioned the three sets of plates and cutlery in the dishwasher."

Charlie hadn't mentioned them because they hadn't struck him as having any significance.

"Breakfast, lunch and dinner?" he hazarded. "Sorry, I didn't look all that closely."

"Nobody eats full meals three times a day these days," said Mike.

"You should talk to some of the body-builders I know."

"I think you can be quite sure, Charlie, that Lydia Perceval didn't go in for weight-training. Actually one of the plates had traces of scrambled egg on it. The other two were big meals, and there were three dessert plates — ice-cream, I think."

"Right," said Charlie equably. "I missed that. She had someone in for a meal, either at mid-day or in the evening."

"I think so. And if it was dinner they left early. Or perhaps they murdered her, faked a forced entry, then took their leave."

"Unlikely, since their finger-prints would be everywhere," said Charlie. "You could hardly keep your gloves on all evening. And that faked forced entry —"

"Yes?"

"Doesn't seem to have gone to a lot of trouble over it, does he?"

"No," agreed Oddie. "There's a ridge of earth on the top of the sill, as if he'd just raised a boot from inside the house and wiped it down."

"Proving it wasn't an arthritic pensioner anyway."

"Was he pushed for time? Was he half-hearted about it because he thought there was no way this could be brought back to him? Or is there some other reason why he hardly bothered to make it convincing?"

"In other respects he was so careful: he put back the phone, turned the milk off on the hot-plate."

"We don't *know* he did either of those things," Oddie pointed out, congenitally cautious. "She may herself have forgotten to turn the milk on. It would be a sensible precaution in the murderer to turn it off, if he didn't want the body found too soon: there could have been a minor fire. And the idea that she was on the phone is just an assumption."

As if on cue the phone rang. Mike Oddie raised his eyebrows at Charlie and picked it up.

"Yes?"

There was a moment's silence at the other end.

"Who is that?" an uncertain female voice asked.

"This is the police."

"Oh, don't say it's true!" The woman's voice cracked with anguish. "She's not dead, is she?"

Oddie registered the concern bordering on hysteria. So this woman whom they had been dissecting as cool, self-contained, was capable of inspiring affection, was she?

"Would you mind telling me who I'm talking to?"

"Dorothy Eccles. I had lunch with her only yesterday!"

"With? —"

"With Lydia. Lydia Perceval. Someone just came on duty here and said they'd heard on the car radio that she was dead, and foul play was suspected. It was a bit fuzzy and they weren't quite sure it was Lydia. Is it true?"

"I'm afraid Mrs Perceval is dead. The circumstances point to murder."

Self-stranglings and accidental stranglings being rare, he said to himself.

"Oh God! Poor Lydia. Was it some intruder?"

"Things are in their early stages as yet. We've come to no conclusions. You say you had lunch with Mrs — was it Mrs?"

"She'd been married, but she reverted to her maiden name. She called herself Mrs Perceval, if pressed."

"You had lunch with Mrs Perceval yester-day?"

"Yes. So happy she was."

"You are? —"

"A librarian. At the British Museum at Boston Spa. We mostly do inter-library loans and international ones, but there is a small readers' area which was very convenient for Lydia. She used to come over at least once a month."

"I see. You say she was happy."

"Yes. Happy in her personal life. There were two boys she had become interested in."

Oddie's antennae twitched.

"Relations?"

"Oh no, I don't think so. No, she'd just got to know them. Local boys — from the village, I think."

"You don't remember their names?"

"Oh dear . . . Colin was one. The other was something very ordinary. Lydia was greatly taken with them. Talked about leaving them something in her will."

"Really?"

"Yes, she was. She intended calling in on her solicitor in Halifax on the way home. I gathered it was all arranged."

"Her solicitor — you don't remember his name?"

"I don't think she told me. I do remember

she mentioned Halifax."

Mike Oddie mouthed "solicitor" at Charlie, and pointed towards the filing cabinet. They had already noted that various sorts of correspondence were stored there under a variety of business-like headings.

"You don't know anything about her relatives?"

"She had a sister in the village — a sister and a brother-in-law."

"Really? Do you know their names?"

"Thea is the sister. . . . I don't remember the surname, but something rather comic-sounding. . . . The brother-in-law is, well, unsatisfactory. Unemployed, I think, and he has a drink problem."

Why don't you just say he drinks too much, Mike wondered?

"You can't remember anything else?"

"She'd had a visit from her nephew over the weekend. Thea's son. He was one of the boys who . . ." She seemed to catch herself up. "Well, Lydia was always very fond of her two nephews. The other one is dead, and she said Maurice was being dragged down by a very common wife. Lydia had very high standards — for herself, but also for others."

Mike Oddie raised his eyebrows. He could guess what having high standards for others meant: snobbishness and censoriousness.

"I see," he said neutrally. "There's nothing else you can remember?"

"No." The voice broke, as if the fact of the murder suddenly caught up with her again. "It's so dreadful . . . I'd like to give all the help I can. . . . We didn't as a rule talk about personal things, you know. Not family or things like that. I knew Lydia as a writer. I used to help her in her research — just in my humble way, of course. I was never a research assistant or anything grand like that. But what we usually talked about was whatever subject she had on the stocks at that moment."

"Charles the tenth."

"Charles the tenth, at this particular time. Oh dear, that's a book that never will be finished. And it was going so well."

"Well, you've been very helpful, Mrs —"

"Miss."

"Miss Eccles. I may need to talk to you again, and if I do I can get in touch with you at the library, I suppose?"

"Yes . . . Such a loss. It's like a light going out."

Mike Oddie heard her gulp and put the phone down. He shook his head and turned to Charlie, who was brandishing a file.

"Oliver Marwick, of Marwick, Chester and Jones. It's Halifax 271463."

Mike was already dialling as he spoke.

"Good morning, this is the police. I need to speak to Oliver Marwick urgently . . . Mr Marwick? West Yorkshire CID here. I believe you had a visit yesterday from Mrs Lydia Perceval."

"No, as a matter of fact she didn't make it." The voice at the other end of the line was cool and lawyerly. Clearly he had not been listening to his radio.

"Do you know why not?"

"She failed to turn up. She got caught up in her research. It's the only thing that can make Lydia unreliable. But why? —"

"How do you know she got caught up in her research?"

"Because she rang me last night. Look, before I answer any more questions, why are you asking me about this?"

"Mrs Perceval was found dead this morning."

"Dead!"

Mike felt he was in a play, and effortlessly hauled up the clichés.

"Foul play is definitely suspected. What time did she ring you last night, Mr Marwick?"

"Just before the news. A minute or two before ten. I know because I was rather — oh, my God!"

"What?"

"She . . . rang off, you see. The line went dead. And I was rather glad, because there was something I wanted to hear about on the news — compensation for haemophiliacs given blood infected with AIDS. I thought she might ring back, but she didn't, and I saw the item. I thought . . . well, I just thought someone had come in."

"I see. Was that likely? Would someone just come in like that to the cottage?"

"Well, I imagine they might. We aren't — weren't personally friendly, but I know she has a sister living in Bly. Thea Hoddle, her name is. I just thought someone like that had dropped in."

"Mr Marwick, how exactly did the phone call end?"

"I'm trying to remember. . . . She seemed to be about to make a new appointment. She said something like 'When can we meet?'"

"Yes?"

"Then . . . then there was a pause . . . I'm trying to remember. She said 'What's that?' as if she was surprised — perhaps by a noise. Then she said 'But'."

"'But'? As if she was surprised by something she saw or heard?"

"Yes. Surprised, or perhaps uncertain. Bewildered, maybe. Then she said something like 'Rob'."

"'Rob'?"

"Yes. With a sort of question in her voice. The voice going upwards, uncertainly. I took it to be a person, but perhaps it was 'robbers' or something like that."

"Yes. Anything more?"

"No. That's when the line went dead."

And Lydia Perceval too, not long afterwards, thought Mike Oddie grimly.

CHAPTER 10

When she was told by a fresh-faced constable of the death of her sister Thea Hoddle swayed, and had to steady herself by clutching at the door jamb. "Are you all right?" the constable asked, not used to conveying such messages, and almost as uncertain and upset as Thea herself. She nodded.

"There'll be a detective along later," said the young man, retreating. "I'd make myself a cup of tea if I were you."

It was kindly-meant advice, and Thea took it, going through the motions in a daze. Pictures of the mature Lydia warred in her mind with pictures of Lydia with her and Andy, on holiday in France, sitting outside a gay little café in Rheims or toiling up Mont St Michel. Emotions were so difficult to disentangle, it was so impossible to say what she felt about her sister.

No, it wasn't. She hated her.

But that was now, and there had been another time, and another Lydia.

Or had that been an illusion, and had there been slumbering inside that gay, sophisticated outside a malignant little beast that was planning to one day steal from her what she valued most?

She drank her tea, standing against the kitchen sink, not wanting to sit in case she broke down. Then she went to the phone and rang the school. Her voice quavering, she told the school secretary what had happened and asked that a message be given to Andy. Then she went into the living room and waited.

She had never wanted more the comforting presence of her husband. But what were they going to say to each other?

Before they left Hilltop Cottage Mike Oddie contacted the Halifax police and spoke to Inspector Harkness, the policeman who had been on the scene when they arrived from Leeds, and who was organising the back-up.

"I'll need someone to guard the cottage," Oddie said.

"I'll have someone there in ten minutes."

"I gather there's a sister and a brother-in-law in the village."

"That's right. Thea and Andy Hoddle their names are. Turn right at the bottom of the hill and it's six houses past The Wheatsheaf. Number sixteen."

"I gather they've been told, then. How did they take it?"

"She. One of our constables spoke to the sister. He said she was very shocked, but he also said he felt there wasn't much grief. He's just a lad and he got away as soon as possible, but the husband's home now, and he spoke to us in the village. He knows how she was killed — they both must by now. With the husband we sensed a shock at the nastiness of it, the violence, but again we felt that there was no great grief. But reactions to news like that can be very deceptive, as I'm sure you know."

"Certainly. Well, we'll get on down there as soon as your man comes."

They left on guard at the cottage the fresh-faced constable who had broken the news to Thea. He looked as if he had just left school, and made Charlie feel very experienced. In the village there was a low-key police operation: two or three men going from house to house asking if anything suspicious had been noticed the night before, or in the days leading up to it. There were no police cars outside number sixteen, but there was a middle-aged woman standing in the bay window looking out. Mike and Charlie got out of the car and looked at the solid, roomy semi-detached with the token gestures towards Tudorality on the upstairs floor.

"Not really in the same class as the cottage,"

murmured Oddie as they pushed open the gate.

"It'd do me," said Charlie.

The door was opened without their knocking, and they introduced themselves to a substantial-looking woman in clothes that had seen better days. Her eyes were red from weeping.

"The death has suddenly hit me," she said, ushering them through. "The manner of it. Andy told me, and it suddenly hit me. So messy and horrible. Lydia would have hated that. She was such a cool, orderly person. This is Andy, my husband."

They were in a living room at the back of the house — a light, airy room with comfortable old furniture. Andy Hoddle was an inch or two shorter than his wife, with a bulky frame and veined cheeks and nose. Mike Oddie was rather surprised to find himself impressed by him, by both of them in fact.

"I'm glad to find you both together," he said.

"Thea phoned the school," Andy Hoddle explained. "Naturally the headmaster agreed I should come home at once."

"You're a schoolmaster?"

Mike kicked himself that he had failed to keep a note of surprise out of his voice. He'd known alcoholic schoolteachers, and it was perhaps surprising that there weren't more. The tiniest of smiles crossed Andy Hoddle's mouth, but it was a bitter one.

"Yes. A recent recruit."

They sat down in capacious armchairs and Charlie got out his notebook.

"Had you seen Mrs Perceval recently?" Mike began.

Andy nodded.

"I took her up a ream of typing paper — when would that be, Thea? — the Saturday before last, I think."

"And you?" Mike Oddie asked, turning to Thea.

"Oh dear — I think it must be nearly a month ago. Maybe more. We met in the village post office. We talked a lot on the phone, of course, but when Lydia was working on a book — writing it, I mean, rather than just researching it — we didn't see much of her. She knew we were there if she needed anything."

"Lydia was something of a local celebrity," put in Andy. "Her books were very well thought of. In the past we used to do things together — holidays, meals out, that sort of thing. But things change, and it wasn't really like that any longer."

"She thought of herself as something of a celebrity?"

152

"I didn't mean that. She usually shunned things like television appearances. . . . I just meant that she had an awful lot to do. Her work was her life."

"I see. . . . There was a photograph of two boys on the bookcase in her study —"

"That would be Gavin and Maurice," said Thea, a shade too quickly. Her eyes had gone to the mantelpiece, where the same picture that Lydia had, the man in naval uniform, gazed out with apparent confidence at the world. "Our sons. That was Gavin when he was working for the Naval Attaché in Washington. Lydia was very fond of Gavin and Maurice — naturally, having no children of her own."

"Of course. Did she keep contact?"

"Gavin is dead." She said it in the flat tone she always had when announcing the fact to strangers. "Maurice works in television in the Midlands, and he keeps in touch with her."

"I see. Now, you say you talked a lot to your sister on the telephone. Had anything of note happened in the last few weeks of her life?"

Andy and Thea looked at each other.

"Her husband had come back," said Andy.

"Our cousin, Jamie Loxton," Thea explained. "He's taken a farm near Kedgely."

"I see. Did this upset her in any way?"

153

"I don't know. I didn't talk to her about it. I don't see why it should. He didn't mean anything to her any longer. It was a very brief marriage."

"How did she learn he was back?"

"He went to tell her. That was rather considerate of him, I think. I know because he dropped in briefly here to say hello when he was in the village a few days ago. It was nice to see him again, though he and I were never close. He said he and Lydia were perfectly polite, and that was that. He'd just thought he ought to tell her he was around again, so she didn't learn it from someone else or run into him accidentally."

"I see. . . . Was there anything else in recent weeks?"

There was a moment's silence.

"There were the Bellingham boys," said Andy carefully.

"Yes, we'd heard about them," said Oddie. "Who were they exactly?"

"Boys from the village. Boys who go to my school actually. Their mother is sick — likely to be so for some time, too, if she really does have M.E. Lydia was giving the boys a meal in the evenings, and generally looking after their welfare."

"I see. Was there any particular reason why she should do this? Was she a close friend of the family?"

"Oh no. They've only recently moved to the village. Somehow or other she'd got to know the boys before their mother's illness was diagnosed."

"Lydia was good with young people," said Thea, again a shade too quickly.

"Well, that solves one mystery," said Oddie. "There were three sets of crockery and cutlery in the dishwasher. Two full sets and some odd plates."

"Probably a full meal for the boys and a snack for herself. Lydia went to Boston Spa yesterday. She has a friend called Eccles in the library there. They may have eaten together."

"Yes, they did. We've talked to Miss Eccles. Tell me, what sort of a woman was your sister?"

Thea was clearly prepared for this question.

"She was a scholar. Very cool, dispassionate. And she loved writing, loved shaping her sentences well, her books well. She was always bookish, even at school, and she got great happiness from her ability to write books herself."

It was hardly what Oddie was interested in. Lydia Perceval's killing could hardly be a result of her scholarship.

"What about her personal life?"

"You could say her books were her personal

life," said Thea. "At least in recent years."

"Yet she'd been married?"

"Briefly, as I said. Jamie was a nice enough boy — man — but he was never very satisfactory." Thea smiled. "Went through jobs like other people go through paper tissues. Andy and I always felt she married him because she couldn't get Robert, his brother."

"You'll find Robert is her heir," said Andy. "She never stopped admiring him."

Something clicked in Oddie's brain.

"Robert Loxton — shouldn't that ring a bell?"

"He's a . . . well, a sort of explorer," said Andy. "Adventurer, if you like. Expeditions, climbs, treks, endurance tests, that sort of thing. Sometimes two-man affairs, with his partner Walter Denning, sometimes altogether more elaborate businesses. He's just finished one in Alaska."

"Right," said Oddie, pleased that the name had meant something to him. "That explains it. Well, you've certainly given us plenty of people we ought to talk to, even if a motive seems still a long way off. Would you say there was anyone — yourselves apart — that Mrs Perceval was especially close to? Someone with whom she might have talked over personal matters?"

They sat thoughtfully for a few moments.

156

"I think Molly Kegan is as likely a person as anyone," said Thea. "She cleaned for Lydia — but she's very intelligent. She worshipped Lydia — admired her very much. And Lydia set a lot of store by her grit and determination. I think she would probably have talked to Molly if she talked to anyone."

"We're going to see Mrs Kegan now," said Oddie, getting up. "She found the body."

"Yes, so Andy tells me. How awful for her! Luckily she's a very strong, self-reliant sort of person." They were at the front door, and Thea pointed across the main street of Bly to a small, rather dreary estate of houses. "She lives over there — third house in."

Mike Oddie thanked them, said their talk had been useful, and that he would very likely be back to them in the course of the investigation. Then he and Charlie walked off in the direction of the Estate.

"Interesting," said Oddie.

"Very," said Charlie. "You say he's been unemployed, but apparently they're reconciled to getting nothing in the will. You'd think they'd at least have hoped for something, and you'd think it would be a kindness in Lydia Perceval to leave them something — if relations between them were as normal as they say."

"He apparently has a 'drink problem,' as

that genteel librarian at Boston Spa calls it. Somehow I don't get the impression that Lydia Perceval would have had much sympathy for a weakness of that kind."

"Then there's the question of the boys, or of Maurice," said Charlie Peace, slowing down to a snail's pace.

"Yes. That *was* interesting. We know he was up for the weekend, and we know that he went to see Lydia, yet nothing was said about it. Only that they 'kept in touch'."

"But you didn't take them up on it?"

"I decided not to — or some instinct told me not to. After all, they could just have shrugged and said that they didn't think it was of importance. On the other hand, if we bring it up next time we talk to them, then we may very well know more about the man and his visit to Lydia, so we may well get more out of them. I bet they're already wondering whether it was wise not to mention the fact that he was here over the weekend."

"Then there was Gavin," said Charlie.

"Ah — you noticed something there?"

"Well, it's just that if you're talking about an old person you can say 'he's dead' and leave it at that, but if you're talking about a young person you'd generally give some sort of explanation: road accident, the illness he was suffering from, or whatever. Unless perhaps it was suicide, or if it was AIDS."

"Right. If we rule out those two, then what are you suggesting?"

"That there was some sort of tension or disagreement between them and Mrs Perceval about the boys. Perhaps that they were competing over them. The photograph in both houses. . . ."

"Right. And you must have noticed how Mrs Hoddle claimed that she talked a lot on the phone to Lydia, and it was only because she was writing that they hadn't seen each other, but she didn't learn about the husband's return from Lydia but from the man himself later. Anyway, that's all speculation. Here we are."

Once again they were expected. The door of the standard, stone-dashed house had a miserable slab of concrete over it. It was open, and in the doorway stood, once again, a woman who had been crying. If Mike Oddie had been forced to put his finger on the difference between the two women he would have said that Thea Hoddle had been crying over what once had been, whereas Mrs Kegan's grief was a present, open wound. She led them through to a pleasant, shabby family living room.

"I'm sorry to be like this," she said, wiping her eyes. "I'm not a weepy sort of person, not as a rule. But I can't get over the shock of finding her like that."

They sat down in easy chairs. Molly Kegan gave a determined gulp and a last dab at her eyes.

"Quite understandable," said Mike. "It was a horrible sight."

"It's not my day for going up there. Mondays and Thursdays I go as a rule. But I had my first raspberries from the garden, and Lydia always loved them, so I took her some up, for her and the boys' dinner. . . . In a way I'm glad I found her. Otherwise it would have been the boys, wouldn't it? I wouldn't wish that on anyone, and certainly not on anyone young."

"That would be the Bellingham boys you're talking about, would it?"

"That's right."

"Would they have a key to the cottage?"

"Oh yes. It had become like a second home to them, because of their mother. You'll have heard about all that from the Hoddles, I expect. Probably a bit slanted. Lydia just loved young people, enjoyed their company, knew she could give them so much. When their mother was ill she naturally shouldered some of her responsibilities. It was the sort of generous thing she would do."

"You admired her very much?"

"Oh, I did. She had . . . well, I'd say distinction is the word. Going up to work for her felt different, somehow. Mind you, the other woman I work for regularly hasn't any conversation except about the telly. Her idea of heaven would be for the BBC to repeat every episode of *All Creatures Great and Small* from beginning to end. You can't have a conversation with a woman like that. You just think your own thoughts and say 'yes' and 'no' occasionally. With Lydia you always had to be on the alert — we'd joke, quarrel even, but we really got on like a house on fire."

"She told you her personal business?"

"On occasion. I wouldn't expect her to, but she might."

"You knew her husband had come back to the area?"

"Oh yes." She smiled a sad, reminiscent smile. "You might say I picked up the pieces."

The two policemen pricked up their ears.

"Really? What exactly do you mean?"

Molly swallowed and spoke carefully.

"The night he came to see her, after he left, she got into a furious rage, throwing things around the room, breaking glass, that kind of thing. A sort of release, I suppose. It was typical of Lydia that she didn't try to clean up, to hide it."

"Why should she be so . . . enraged about

161

her husband coming back to the area?"

"It hadn't been much of a marriage."

"I gathered that — short and unsatisfactory, Mrs Hoddle implied. All the odder that she should fly into such a rage, surely?"

Molly Kegan thought for a moment.

"Lydia didn't like failures. And she didn't like failure. I think she saw the marriage as a failure of her own, and a humiliating one."

"She sounds rather merciless."

"Maybe. But merciless to herself as well."

"Do you know the husband?"

"I've had him pointed out to me in the village. Everyone knows everyone here, and he doesn't live far away. Of course people are interested because he used to be married to Lydia. Looked a pleasant enough chap — young for his age. I've never spoken to him."

"You said earlier that I'd get a slanted view of Lydia and the Bellingham boys from Mrs Hoddle. Why did you say that?"

Mrs Kegan for the first time appeared hesitant. There seemed to be a consciousness that this was something that did not reflect well on Lydia.

"Well, there were their boys, you see."

"Gavin and Maurice?"

"Yes . . . I don't want to be unkind. Thea Hoddle is a perfectly nice woman, and she's had her problems. . . . But of course the boys worshipped their aunt. Naturally they found there the sort of stimulation bright boys need, more than they could get at home."

"But the Hoddles struck me as intelligent people."

She looked at him incredulously.

"But you couldn't compare them with Lydia! Lydia was a writer, she was universally admired! She could rouse the boys' interests, channel them — they blossomed when they were with her."

"I see. Were you working for her then?"

"Oh no. Only the last ten years. But I was living here. And of course all the village knew how fond they were of Lydia, how much they used to go up there."

"I can see this must have upset the parents."

"Yes. They couldn't hide that. They made it a sort of competition, which was silly."

"Was it so silly? If they felt their children slipping away from them?"

"It was silly because they couldn't win," said Molly Kegan brutally. "Lydia had so much more to offer."

It was a subject, clearly, which Molly Kegan was never going to see in a balanced way. Oddie shifted ground.

"What about the Bellingham boys?"

"What about them? They gave Lydia a very happy last few weeks of her life, I know

163

that. She loved helping them, bringing them on." She added, as if scoring a debating point: "And the father was as pleased as punch about it."

"Oh?"

"He was boasting in The Wheatsheaf last night about how his boys had been made quite pets of by the 'writer lady up the hill.' Said she'd been down to talk to him about them."

"Really? Last night, you say? How do you know?"

"How does anyone know anything in a village? Someone told me. Someone whose husband was there."

"Obviously we're going to have to talk to the Bellinghams," said Mike Oddie, getting up and signalling to Charlie that the interview was at an end. "The boys probably saw more of her in recent days than anyone else. Oh, by the way, the nephew was up over the weekend, wasn't he?"

"Oh yes. *And* his wife. She caused more interest in the village than he did."

"Why was that?"

"Because she used to be Sharon Turner in *Waterloo Terrace*."

"Her with the tight short skirts?" asked Charlie, the glint of lust in his eye.

"Yes. Pretty much the same off-screen as

on it, so they say. They kept her away from Lydia."

"Oh?"

"Wise of them. The one time they met Lydia said her language was unprintable. Lydia was very sensitive to language, and she hated vulgarity or crudeness. Maurice went up to see her, but Kelly stayed down here."

"And was Lydia pleased to see him?"

"I haven't spoken to her since. On Monday — yesterday — I went up but she was in Boston Spa, doing work on her book. I had the key to come and go as I like. That's how I came to go up there this morning and —"

Her face crumpled. The two policemen made their excuses and left. As they made towards the car Oddie said:

"That was a rather different view of the woman to the one we formed in the cottage. Would you say she was reliable?"

"I'd say she was in love," said Charlie.

CHAPTER 11

The village of Bly, which to the policemen had seemed at first sight no more than a street on either side of a crossroad, turned out on closer acquaintance to have rather more ramifications than that. The small council estate on which Molly Kegan lived and brought up her children swelled the population by a hundred or so, and when one walked it one realized that the main street had sprouted appendages: a crescent of semis nestled behind the pub, two or three stumps of roads leading to nowhere were bordered by pre-and postwar family housing. Even so Mike Oddie estimated that the number of souls living within the village area would amount to well under a thousand.

"The new sheriff and his deputy come to town," murmured Charlie as they turned again into the main street. "And everyone waits, and watches, and wonders."

"Nonsense — we're the FBI," said Oddie. "Sent to the Deep South and wondering what makes people tick there. What say we take half an hour off for a pint, and see if there is any village gossip to be gleaned?"

But when he turned his head in Charlie's direction he saw that something else had seized the constable's attention.

"Someone wants to talk to us," he said.

In a town the incidence of murder might have brought little knots of people onto street corners to watch the police with unconcealed interest, even occasionally to offer information and advice. A village was different. In this one the people had kept to their own houses, communicating and commenting on the intelligence by telephone, and watching the police activity from darkened rooms with field-glasses, or through cracks produced by infinitesimally opening their front doors. If they had legitimate business outside the house they scuttled about it in an embarrassed fashion, as if afraid of being accused by their neighbours of showing vulgar curiosity. But the boy Charlie had his eye on was perhaps too young to have absorbed village mores, or perhaps he simply didn't care about them: he was around thirteen, afflicted by the sort of facial blemishes that television advertisements claim to be able to remove as if by magic, and eating avidly from a packet of crisps. He was watching them with interest, and with a concentrated expression that suggested he was trying to make up his mind.

"Now," wondered Charlie aloud, "will he

talk more openly to you because you're white, or to me because I'm more his age?"

The question was only answered indirectly. As they approached on the other side of the road the boy made a decision: he crossed the road and went up to Mike Oddie.

"My mum says you ought to talk to her."

"Oh?" The two policemen stopped, and Mike looked down at the blemished, heavy-featured face. "Why is that? Does she have any special information about the murder?"

"Well, not *special*, I don't think. But like she says, if you run the village post office everyone comes in and you hear everyone's news. My mum says there's nothing goes on in Bly but what she knows about it. . . . Though a lot of it's not very interesting," the boy concluded lamely but honestly.

"Well, maybe we'll just drop in on your mother," said Mike Oddie, thinking this might be an alternative to pub gossip. "The post office is — where?"

"Oh, it's not a real post office — just a shop with a post office counter," said the boy. "Come on, I'll show you." He walked self-importantly along the main street, decidedly pleased with his own prominence. When they got to the door of the general-store-cum-post-office, with the name M. Wetherby over the door, the boy pointed Oddie inside and then threw a glance in Charlie's direction which said as clearly as words: Don't you go with him. I've got something to tell you.

"Oh, it's the police, is it? Well, you've come to the right place, I'll say that for you." The voice started the moment Oddie set foot over the shop's threshold. It proceeded from a fleshy woman in an unwisely summery dress, from which her flabby arms protruded like a string of pink grapefruit. Her accent was not northern but her voice had a staying power that made the heart sink. This, presumably, was M. Wetherby. "Well, we can't talk here. Never know who might come in. Come into my back room: with the door closed you can't hear nothing out here. You too, young man" — for Charlie had lurked on the pavement outside, intending to have a private session with the woman's son — "you'll be needed to take notes. Jason — mind the shop."

"Mum, do I have to? You know I'm not supposed to do any of the post office stuff —"

"Bugger post office regulations." She waddled ahead into the back room built on as an extension to the shop and post office. "He's off school with an upset tummy. No reason why he shouldn't make hisself useful. Now, what was it you wanted to know? She wasn't liked, you know. That's not to say there wasn't plenty as admired her, or talked her up, because it was something to have a famous writer in the village, or just outside it, and those that read her books said she told a good tale, for all it was true, not fiction, which is where my tastes lie. But liked she was not. Well, it's not surprising, is it? She'd nothing in common with us, not the ordinary people of the village, and if she exchanged the time of day with us that was as much as she would do." She put on her idea of an upper-class drawl: "'Mrs Wetherby, my publishers sent off my proofs three days ago and they're not here yet,' she'd say to me, though I'd tell her time and time again that delivery comes from Halifax and in't nothing to do with me. Always very snooty she was when she came down into the village, as if living in three cottages thrown together gave you lady-of-the-manor rights, I ask you. But that's not to say that one of us would do a thing like that to her, naturally we wouldn't, we was proud of her in a way, no, the obvious place you've got to look — and I'm sure you don't need me to tell you — is the village newcomers. Well, it stands to reason, don't it, she lives here year after year and nothing happens to her, and suddenly they move in and she's done in, not that I've anything against the boys themselves, they've been in here and been polite enough, as polite as boys *are* these days, and standards have gone down as we all know, and Jason says that they're not disliked at school, for all they've begun boasting to their mates about being left money, which puts other boys' backs up as I'm sure you'll understand. But the mother is a poor thing, there's nobody can say different to that, without a sparkle of life in her, and the father, for all his noise and bluster, is nothing but a braggart and a boozer, and I know the type, because I had a braggart and a boozer for a husband, God's pity on the woman as has to put up with him now, for woman there must be, because he has a way with him —"

"Pad run out," said Charlie, snapping his notebook shut and making for the door. "I'll get another one from the car."

That was enough time to waste on that woman, he thought, as he made his escape. She was nothing but a leaky mouth, one who blabbed on autocue. That was interesting, though, what she said about the boys boasting at school — if it was true, and if it was money from Lydia. Still, Oddie could pick up jewels like that from the garbage without his notebook at the ready. The boy was someone who should be questioned while he was still willing to talk.

There were no customers in the shop, or at the post office counter. Jason was just standing there, bored. But he brightened up when Charlie came through the door.

"She thinks she knows everything, but she don't," he said, nodding contemptuously towards the door. "She just talks and never listens."

"Can be useful at times, I suppose," said Charlie.

The boy thought ponderously, then nodded.

"Like I can say 'I told you' and not be telling a lie? Yes, well that works sometimes. Only there's some things she always does manage to hear."

"Oh? Like if you tell her where you're going to be in the evening, and she finds out you weren't?"

"Yeah . . . How did you guess?"

"Not difficult. Where did you say you'd be last night?"

"Said I was doing homework with Garry Mathers."

"And you weren't?"

"Well, I *was*. I mean I went there, in case anything was said, or questions asked. We always go upstairs to Garry's bedroom, and Mrs Mathers has the telly on loud downstairs, so she never knows when I leave the house."

"So where did you and your girlfriend go?"

"Up the — how did you know?"

He really was a very slow boy. Still, often

the best witnesses were stupid.

"I know. I remember what I did at your age. So you went up the hill, did you?"

"Yes, I did. I went past Mrs Perceval's house, but I didn't notice anything. Don't suppose I looked. Then I met me girlfriend in the little wood near the gravel pit — by arrangement, like."

"I see. What time was this?"

"I went up about quarter past eight, near enough. It was getting dark when we came away — about half past nine, I suppose. I know I was home well before ten."

"Was it as you both came down the hill that you noticed something?"

The boy's lip curled.

"No, we came down separately. We're not daft. Julie took the back path, and I took the road past the cottage. They notice everything in this place. . . . No, it was earlier, while we were up in the woods, like."

He shuffled and picked at a spot. Julie, thought Charlie, must be hard up.

"I suppose you were . . . down in the undergrowth," he suggested. "Not very visible."

"'Course we were! Practically burrowed in. We weren't trying to hide, and maybe he wasn't either. But it was just where he put his car, like."

"Where he put his car?" said Charlie, repressing impatience.

"Yes, he drove it up the path towards the pit and left it in the little clearing there. He could easily have left it by the road — it's wide enough. But he drove it into the wood."

"You say he. That means you saw him?"

"Yes. We — well, we just stayed and watched him. He got out of the car —"

"What sort of car?"

"Ford Fiesta. Dark blue. We looked at it as we left."

"Number plate?"

"Don't remember. But it was F reg."

"Right. Sorry I interrupted."

"Well, there's not much more. He got out, shut and locked the doors, and walked down the path towards the road."

"What did he look like?"

"I didn't see his face full on, only sideways. He had a beard — a dark, bushy one."

"That's interesting. What sort of height was he?"

"Fairly tall, I'd say. Going on six foot."

"Clothing?"

"Wore a dark shirt, open at the neck. And jeans."

"Any guess at his age?"

"Didn't see him well enough. He wasn't grey, and he walked like he was pretty fit and active."

"I see. And when you went past the cottage, did you look at it the second time?"

"Yes, I did. It's the only house before you get back to the village, so I thought he might have gone there. But he'd left the woods ten minutes or so by then. There were lights on at Hilltop Cottage, but I couldn't see anyone or anything unusual there. Wasn't all that interested — *then*."

The door to the little back sitting room began to open gradually. "I'm afraid we really have a great deal to do," Charlie heard. He's giving up — thinks I should have got all I need, he thought. She's nothing but a time-waster. But as the judgment went through his mind he heard Mrs Wetherby say:

"You'll be talking to the husband, I dare say?"

She was standing, wobbling gently, in the doorway.

"I expect so," said Mike Oddie, clearly ready for a hurried departure. "Though since we gather that they'd been divorced for many years —"

"Why come back here, that's what I'd like to know? She couldn't explain that."

"Who couldn't?"

"His girlfriend. Runs the post office and shop up at Kedgely, so naturally we're in touch now and then, and we've met at a P.O.

175

course in Halifax. I knew what sort *he* was as soon as she started talking about him: drifter, wastrel, sponger — *that's* the sort he is, for all she puts it nicely and says he's 'never found his niche.' *Niche!* Who does find their bloody niche? I wouldn't say my niche was a shop-cum-post-office, but I have to buckle down and make a go of it, don't I?" The chins wobbled with self-righteousness. "Oh no, I'd got him summed up, for all he's got a beard and goes striding through the place looking so macho. He's what Australians call a no-hoper — a walking lost cause. Some women go for that, but not me. If I'm going to throw meself into the sea of matrimony I'll attach meself to a life-boat, not a concrete block!"

"I'm sure you will," said Oddie, smiling his goodbyes in the interval of a caught breath and escaping through the door. "Next problem: find a life-boat that wants to be attached to a quivering mass of talkative jelly," he muttered to Charlie as they marched down the street towards their car.

"Still, there were a couple of things of interest, even in the bits I heard," Charlie had to concede. "The boys talking about the will at school —"

"Yes, that was interesting. I pressed her after you'd gone, during a brief pause, and it was money from Lydia Perceval that they were boasting about. What was the other thing?"

"The husband having a beard."

"Oh? Why that?"

"The boy — Jason — was up in the wood just beyond the cottage yesterday evening with his girlfriend. A man with a beard drove his car into the wood and left it in a clearing there — round about quarter, twenty past nine."

"Ah — did the boy recognise him?"

"No. Only saw him side-face. But the husband only seems to have been around the village once or twice, probably in daytime, so it's quite possible he wouldn't."

"Interesting. Or possibly the usual red herring one gets in murder cases and all he wanted was a pee."

"Definitely not that, anyway. The kid says he strode towards the road. Of course he could have been having it off with a married woman in the village here —"

Their hands were on the door-handles of their car when they heard an "I say!" and turned to see an overweight man emerging from a rather shoddy-looking semi-detached on the fringe of the village. He came up to them with an air of bluster and self-importance which was far from ingratiating.

"They tell me you're the policemen on the murder case."

"That's right," said Mike, with more geniality than he felt.

"Then you'll want to talk to me and my boys. We must have been among the last to see her."

"Ah yes. You must be Mr Bellingham."

"Nick Bellingham." He held out his hand, which was surprisingly sweaty. "Glad to meet you. My boys were up with her last evening, and she came down with them — to make herself known, so to speak."

"You hadn't met her?"

"Oh no — last night was the first time."

"Nor your wife?"

"No, the friendship was with the boys. She'd been champion since their mother's illness was diagnosed. Soon as I heard of the murder I begged the rest of the day off work — I was appalled. Terrible tragedy. Unthinkable. I phoned the headmaster at the boys' school, and he was going to break it to them. I didn't say they should come home specially — was I right?"

"Quite right. We have a great deal of routine stuff to get through. But if we could talk to them this evening?"

"No problem," said Bellingham, rubbing his hands. "What's the drill? Do I make myself scarce?"

"No, no — not at all. This will just be a

routine session, but one of the parents should be present. Till this evening then."

But as they drove away, Oddie said to Charlie: "If it should turn out that one of the boys, or both of them, are involved, then some other way of questioning them will have to be found."

"Headmaster or something?"

"Yes, and each boy separately."

"He was odd, wasn't he?" said Charlie thoughtfully. "Somehow the words and manner didn't go together, and the words of regret were an afterthought. He seemed to be enjoying it."

"He was. But then people do. People a lot more intelligent than him."

"Or than he seemed," amended Charlie. "One of the things you learn growing up in Brixton is to seem to the police to be a lot thicker than you really are."

"You may be right. Though I sensed a true-blue homegrown thickness in Mr Bellingham. Not that I'm prejudging matters: I've known plenty of stupid murderers — and sometimes they murder for stupid reasons, and sometimes for perfectly good ones like money or sex."

"Still, there's no reason to suspect Bellingham, is there?"

"None at all, except that he was one of the last to see her alive, and later left his house and was seen in the pub."

"She was being good to his boys and getting him off the hook of looking after them. You could say he had a sort of anti-motive."

"You could, if you weren't trying to keep a totally open mind."

For the rest of the afternoon they were busy with the sort of petty routine that proliferates in a murder case beyond even the day-to-day pettinesses of police routine. Oddie did manage to fax the Anchorage police, hoping to get a message through to Lydia's cousin and heir, and he phoned Lydia's solicitor again and eventually managed to get out of him the sums she had been planning to leave to the two boys. Charlie meanwhile checked up on the work of the uniformed men who had been doing door-to-door enquiries in the village. Little seemed to have emerged beyond the fact that Lydia was not a familiar figure in Bly, though the village people had been mildly proud to have her among them. They had been more interested in the visit of Kelly Marsh from *Waterloo Terrace*, and it was agreed that she and her husband had packed up their car the night before, and had left with their baby son soon after eight that morning.

As they drove back to Bly Mike Oddie said:

"We'll keep the questions mainly to factual, neutral matters. We've got no substantial grounds for suspicion, and we don't want to put them on their guard."

"No substantial grounds? You mean beyond the codicil?"

"Beyond the codicil," agreed Mike Oddie. "Which was never signed, but which should have been signed yesterday. That codicil, by the bye, could give a motive to the father as well as the boys: he may have felt that one way or another he could get his hands on the money, both of them being minors. Even in an age of high inflation ten thousand pounds is not to be sneezed at."

"I'm not sneezing," said Charlie. "But did he know about it? Telling your father is not quite the same thing as telling your mates at school."

"True. Anyway that's one thing I shall have to bring up, without making a big issue out of it."

Oddie went thoughtful until, minutes later, Charlie pulled up outside the Bellingham home. Their first ring brought Nick to the door, still shining with sweat and exuding bluffness and eagerness to please. He ushered them through the hall and into the living room. Mike Oddie's antennae quivered: he had lived alone for some years after the death of his first wife, and he knew the feel of a room hastily and inexpertly cleaned and tidied

181

in anticipation of a visit. This room had it. But then that was very much to be expected, when the housewife/mother had recently been taken off to hospital.

"Sorry about the mess," said Nick Bellingham unnecessarily. "I'm thinking of getting that Mrs Kegan in, while the wife's poorly."

Mike and Charlie were put into a pair of armchairs facing the two boys, seated side by side on a sofa. It was all rather unreal, like a television set for a prestige detective series. The boys' appearance also struck the two detectives as incongruous: what boy these days wears a necktie around the house after school? Ted and Colin wore flannels and white shirts, and like the room had the air of being newly scrubbed and tidied. They also had an air of sadness tinged, Oddie felt — but wouldn't it be the same with any boys? — with excitement.

"Ted," said Nick Bellingham, gesturing. "And Colin."

"Hello," the two boys said.

"Right," said Oddie, settling down in his chair and putting on his friendliest face. "Could you tell me how long you had known Mrs Perceval?"

"Just a matter of weeks," said Ted.

"How did you meet her?"

"We didn't exactly meet her. . . . We go

182

up the hill there to practise speed cycling on the open space near the gravel pit. She spoke to us one day, then we stopped to chat to her, then it — well, it went on from there."

"I see. You seem to have got quite close very quickly. Why do you think that was?"

"We just clicked," said Colin. "Somehow."

Mike's antennae quivered again, but what were they reacting to? Perhaps the tone of the reply: there was a trace of smugness, of the smart-alec, in the voice.

"It was quite natural really," said Ted. "She didn't have any children, but she'd been very fond of her nephews. They'd grown up, one of them had died — in the Falklands War, actually —"

"Ah."

"— so she, well, she didn't really have anybody."

"You were sort of replacements for the nephews?"

"Well, in a way. Though it didn't feel like that."

"And on your side?"

There was a moment's silence, then Nick Bellingham spoke, from his upright chair at the table.

"It was their mother, you see. She'd been ill for months and we hadn't realized it. I blame myself, I make no bones about that.

She'd been sort of fading away, and I just got ratty at her. I'd never even heard of M.E. — I'm no great reader. And of course I'm out at work all day — sometimes half the evening too. . . ."

"You mean the boys had had little home life?" Oddie asked, easily.

"Not to put too fine a point on it, yes," said Bellingham, with his customary fondness for cliché.

"But we liked her," said Ted eagerly. "She was really interesting, wasn't she, Colin? She knew such a lot, and it was unusual her being a writer."

"You felt you learned a lot just being there," said his brother.

"I'm sure you did," said Oddie. "And when your mother was taken into hospital she provided a base for you in the evenings?"

"Yes. We got her to the doctor's last week, and he put her in immediately. That's when Mrs Perceval made her offer. We went there after school, and she cooked an evening meal for us."

"And that's what happened last night?"

"Yes." A catch came into Ted's voice. "I can't believe that just after we saw her. . . ."

"Let's stick to what happened last night. Did you go up to Hilltop Cottage straight after school?"

"No, we went swimming in the Halifax baths first. We got to the cottage around six, and Lydia — Mrs Perceval — cooked us steak and chips."

"What did you talk about?"

The boys looked at each other, screwing up their faces.

"I remember we talked about being a vegetarian, and how we didn't like our steak too red and fleshy," said Ted.

"Was Mrs Perceval a vegetarian?" Charlie asked.

"Oh no. She was a red meat and fur coat sort of person," said Colin.

"She was a bit old-fashioned in a lot of ways," said Ted.

"Did you come straight home after the meal?"

"No, we played Monopoly. Then we said we'd be getting back, and Mrs Perceval said she'd come down with us."

Oddie nodded, and looked serious.

"Now, you were alone in the house, were you?"

"Oh yes."

"Quite sure?"

"Yes. Well — unless there was some kind of intruder."

Ted shivered. This was something he had not thought about before, apparently.

"Right. So you left the cottage. Did Mrs Perceval lock up?"

"Yes, she locked up and put the key in her handbag."

"Did she say why she was going down to the village with you?"

"To meet Dad," said Ted.

"And to make sure which house we lived in," added Colin.

"No other reason as well?"

"I don't think so. Not that she said."

"Did anything happen on your way here?"

"Not really," said Ted, thinking. "We went past her sister's house, and she commented on her nephew still being here. His car was parked outside."

"She'd had a row with him over the week-end," said Colin.

"We don't *know* that," said Ted, turning on him.

"What makes you think it?" asked Charlie.

"We came in when he was up there," said Colin, still with that rather-pleased-with-himself tone. "There was a sort of atmosphere. She was sort of — well, like she'd lost her cool."

"Normally she was a very cool person," said Ted.

"I think it was what people mean when they say someone is 'ruffled'," said Colin. "Later

186

on, after he'd gone, she made remarks — sort of snide remarks — about him."

"For instance?"

"Like that he'd thrown his chances away, and that he'd married the sort of woman who would drag him down. We thought it was rather exciting that he was in television, and she didn't like that."

"She'd have liked it even less if she'd seen you trying to catch a glimpse of Sharon from *Waterloo Terrace* from our bedroom window on Saturday morning," said Ted wickedly.

"Well, it's not often you see telly people in Bly," Colin pointed out. "And she's really page three!"

"Right," said Oddie, "so you came along to this house. What happened?"

"She just said hello," said Nick Bellingham, seeming rather embarrassed. "The house was in a bit of a mess, couldn't really invite her in, but she didn't want that. She just — well, she said hello and went."

"I think it was just so she knew who Dad was," said Ted.

"What time was this?"

"Oh — maybe a quarter to ten," said Ted, after a moment's thought. "We watched the end of *Taggart,* and then it was news time. We don't watch the news if Dad isn't in, so we switched it off and went upstairs to do

187

our homework."

"You weren't in, then?" Oddie asked Nick.

"I slipped out for a quick pint as soon as the lads were home," their father said. "I'd been doing the firm's paperwork all evening, and I was parched."

"But would you agree about times?"

"The boys would be right about that. I'd had my head over account books all evening, so I hadn't seen any television. I'm hazy about time at the best of times."

"Did you see Mrs Perceval in the street when you went to the pub?"

"No — I'd spent a minute or two with the boys before I went out, asked them what they'd been doing and so on."

"But as far as you know," said Oddie, turning back to the boys, "she went straight back to the cottage."

"I suppose so," said Colin slowly. "As we said, she didn't say she was going to do anything else. I suppose she could have gone to see her sister."

"Don't be daft," cut in Ted. "Not with Kelly Marsh there. She said she'd walk miles to avoid bumping into her again."

"Is there anyone else she might have visited?"

"There's her cleaner, Mrs Kegan. She was very fond of her."

"But why would she?" asked Colin. "She'd been to the cottage yesterday. She was there when we phoned to say we were going swimming. Why do you think she called on anyone?"

"I don't. I'm just checking. She would only have had time to pop in for a few words at most."

Colin looked at him, sharp-eyed.

"Does that mean you know what time she was killed?"

"She rang someone just before ten." Mike Oddie decided to opt for vagueness. Boys' imaginations could make something nightmarish of that last telephone conversation. "We think it was around then that she was killed."

"Well, whoever did it, hanging's too good for them," said Nick Bellingham, with that heartiness the bluff Britisher always assumes when hanging or flogging is in question. "She'd been wonderful to the boys — a real saint."

Oddie doubted it, but didn't share his doubts.

"Well, I think that's all for now," he said, getting up and making for the door. "Though there'll probably be more questions when we've got the picture clearer in our minds. I'm sorry to have to do this," he said turning to the boys. "I realise it must be distressing.

You must have got fond of her."

"We did," said Ted. "It was good to have someone interested in us and what we did."

"She certainly seems to have been fond of you," said Oddie. "You know she intended to leave you both some money?"

The boys responded simultaneously.

"Money?" said Ted.

"Intended?" said Colin.

CHAPTER 12

More people were talking or thinking about Lydia Perceval in Bly that evening than ever talked or thought about her in life. It seemed there was only one possible subject of conversation, and conjecture ranged from the fantastical to the plain ignorant. The people of Bly were on the whole sensible people, however, and they laughed at the woman who, showing an imperfect grasp of the practicalities, suggested that Lydia had committed suicide. And they were sceptical too of the suggestion that she had been the victim of a fatwah: the reasons adduced, that she was a writer, and had written a book on Lawrence of Arabia, they found unimpressive. None of the people who knew her best doubted it was murder or that it had had one of the usual motives for murder. They talked the matter over in tones that were hushed, uncertain, but not, except in one case, grief-stricken.

Over a late-night whisky, their first of the day, Andy and Thea Hoddle mulled over things yet again, alcohol seeming to illumine more sharply the nature of their dilemma.

"I don't know why we didn't mention their

being here," said Andy, his forehead creased in self-criticism. "It's not as though we talked it over and came to a rational decision."

"We can say they never asked us," said Thea.

"We can say that. I don't think they'll buy it. After all the subject of the boys — our boys — came up, and we just said that Maurice worked for Midlands Television. It would have been natural. . . ."

"Yes . . ." Thea looked down into her glass. It was so seldom that they discussed Maurice. "I suppose it was just the thought that Lydia had been murdered, and Maurice had gone out last night."

"Yes. He said he was going to see if there were any of his old school-friends in the pub. He didn't tell you if he'd met any?"

Thea shook her head.

"No. I suppose he did go to The Wheatsheaf?"

"Please God he did. We can hardly go and ask."

"It may come up in conversation — there'd have been plenty of men from the village in there. . . . Eventually the police are going to be asking."

"They're going to be asking about Kelly too."

"I don't see that Kelly had anything to do

with Lydia. The fact that they disliked each other when they met is hardly relevant, since they only met once. As far as we know she was in bed getting her beauty sleep, as she called it."

"They're going to be asking about us too." Thea shook her head.

"And that's going to be just as unsatisfactory. As far as you know I was upstairs reading in bed, at least if she was killed late evening, as the village is saying. And as far as I know you were down here watching the ten o'clock news. We know each other so well we know there's no possibility of the other lying. But *they* don't."

"The question is," said Andy, swallowing the last of his Scotch and getting up to pour himself another, "do we go along tomorrow and say: 'Oh, by the way, we forgot to say our son was staying with us that night'?"

"It's going to look bad," said Thea. "It's going to look as if Maurice being here was — well — relevant. Something important."

"It's going to look bad however it comes up," Andy pointed out. "And it's my guess they know already they were here. You know what Bly is like. And Kelly being in the village was a five-day wonder even before the murder."

"Maurice didn't say anything on the

phone?" Thea asked.

"Just 'Good Lord!' and later that if he'd been asked he would have said that Lydia would die gracefully at a great age and in full possession of her faculties."

"But he said he'd come to the funeral?"

"Yes." Andy grinned. "He also said he thought that Lydia would have agreed to dispense with Kelly's presence."

"Well, that's true enough . . . though it makes public what they thought of each other."

"I'm sure everyone in Bly has known that all along. Lydia was not backward in giving her opinion — and neither is Kelly, come to that. . . . It's what Maurice thought of Lydia that worries me."

"Yes. It's not just his having gone out last night, is it? Or the fact that they seem to have had some sort of minor quarrel when he went up there. It's that sense of . . . of bottled-up resentment I got whenever we talked of her."

"Yes. Kelly felt it too, you know."

"I know. She told me he always goes tense when the subject of his aunt comes up."

"Maybe — I don't know — maybe it's a feeling that Lydia *used* them, him and Gavin. I wish it was something he was willing to discuss. He pretended on the surface to be so relaxed about her — rather cynical and seeing through her. And yet underneath I got the feeling that he . . . well, hated her."

"Yes. Perhaps that's how he's felt since Gavin's death."

"Perhaps it's something he feels on his own behalf."

In the bedroom of number six, High Street, which Ted had occupied since the move North the boys were talking in hushed, urgent tones. They had heard the front door shut minutes before, as their father returned from The Wheatsheaf. He had not been able to resist being the centre of attention as one of the last to speak to the dead woman.

"You really blew it," said Ted scornfully. "You're a right plonker!" He threw his voice into a bitter imitation of his brother. "'Intended?'"

"I don't suppose he noticed," muttered Colin.

"Of course he noticed. He's a policeman."

"Anyway he was bound to find out that we knew. We've talked about it at school."

"*You* talked about it. I never cared about the money."

"Says you!"

"I didn't! I wished we'd never heard about it. I wasn't going up there for that."

"Oh no? Ten thousand quid, and you

'weren't going up there for that'." He produced his own imitation of his brother's tones.
"Who is going to believe that?"

"It's the truth."

"Well, I was, I tell you straight."

"You did a good job sucking up to her."

"Yes, I did."

"She thought you were the brightest of us."

"And she was dead right."

"Oh yes? Then how come the moment the
cop mentions the legacy you let out the fact
that you knew about it? *Intended!*"

Colin, his face red with rage, turned on his
stomach and began maniacally punching the
pillow.

"Yes — not so bright after all, are you?"

"I'm punching that stupid cow's head! I'm
punching her because she never signed that
bleeding will!"

Jamie Loxton sat on the sofa in Fieldhay
Farm near Kedgely, his arm around his
fiancée, the pair of them companionably warm
and close. Mary Scully still slept most nights
over her little shop, and she still hadn't named
a date for marriage, but more and more they
were emerging from, in cant phrase, "having
a relationship," and were becoming a pair.
The living room of Fieldhay Farm was evidence of how well they went together. The

rest of the old farm was cheerless and run-down, just as Jamie had taken it over, but this room, on which they had really worked, was bright and inviting: red and orange cush-ions, warm-coloured rugs, posters and pic-tures around the walls. No great expense had been incurred, and nothing done to prevent it being the living space of a working farmer, but already it felt to them like a real home. Jamie, for once in his life, felt that this was a place in which he belonged.

"I'm glad I saw Lydia once before she died," he said. "It seems in a way to have rounded things off."

"Yes . . . I hope the police will see it like that."

"Well, it was a perfectly amiable meeting. I don't believe Lydia would have told anyone anything to the contrary."

Jamie Loxton had a habit of ignoring un-palatable facts which could explain his blithe progress from disaster to disaster. His fiancée was trying to cure him of it.

"You did say she was trying to niggle you all the time," she said.

"She was. But that's not likely to be some-thing she'll have confided in anyone else, is it? Especially as I conspicuously refused to be niggled. I've learnt to live with my past."

"That's because it is a past," said Mary,

the ring of confidence in her voice. She was very conscious that Jamie was potentially one of her successes. "You've come through all that. This really is a new start."

"Yes . . . I sometimes wonder how far it was Lydia made me what I was. I'd never lost a job when I married her."

"Blame isn't a very productive emotion."

"Stop lecturing! Leave me some illusions! . . . But you're right, of course. You're wasted on me, you know. You should be exercising your wisdom on a wider circle."

"I've done that. I'll settle for you . . . I'm glad we were out together last night. And I'm glad we were *seen*. The police wouldn't have been very impressed if we'd just been here together alone."

"No . . . But I wish we knew when she was killed."

"Well, Mrs Wetherby says it was around ten."

"What Mrs Wetherby says isn't evidence. It isn't even usually true. You always say that with half the gossip she passes on she gets the wrong end of the stick."

"Village postmistresses are not infallible. But the police have talked to her, so I think this is true."

"I hope so, that's all. I don't fancy being suspected. With my sort of record the less attention I get from the police the better I like it."

"You've no actual police record."

"I must have had special protection from God, rather as He is said to protect drunks."

"Anyway, you dropped me off at the shop at ten to ten. That clock on the Methodist Chapel is never wrong. There's no way you could have got to Bly by ten; not on these roads."

"That's all very well, but there's only your word that it was ten to."

"I wouldn't be so sure. If a car comes through Kedgely at night everyone rushes to the window to see who it is. It's that kind of place. Anyway, we came straight here from the White Rose. They'll remember when we left."

"Why on earth should they?"

"We were the last ones in the restaurant, and you made that frightful fuss when you thought you'd lost your car keys."

"Oh, that's right. It's incredible how you can look in a pocket for your keys, and then eventually find they're there after all."

"It's all the other junk you've got in there as well."

"Anyway, I felt a right noodle."

"People do it all the time. You've got to get out of the habit of thinking of yourself as a noodle." She put into her voice a ring of confidence that was stronger than she actually felt. "You'll see: everything will check out. The police will see that you couldn't have done it."

"You're so good for me."

"We're good for each other."

She smiled up at him, and brushed her lips tenderly against his clean-shaven cheek.

In The Wheatsheaf it was well past closing time, and the last of the regulars were nursing the last of their pints of beer. Stan Podmore, the landlord, was busying himself with a succession of closing-down tasks, obviously and noisily.

"Are you going to tell the police about last night?" Jim Scattergood shouted from the other end of the bar, more to delay going home than because he wanted an answer.

"What about last night?"

"About the argy-bargy in here."

"There wasn't any argy-bargy in here."

"Little confrontation — whatever you like to call it. 'Course, I couldn't mention it while that Bellingham man was here. . . ."

Stan Podmore came over and pointed a fat finger at his customer.

"Look here, Jim Scattergood, there wasn't any argy-bargy and there wasn't any confrontation. Bellingham was sounding off about how Mrs Perceval had taken his boys under her wing, and what a good thing it was, and how she'd just been down to talk things over with him, and young Hoddle went over and said something to him. That was all that happened. If you call that an argument you've got an over-vivid imagination."

"You didn't hear what Hoddle said?"

"No, I didn't. Hardly anything. Bellingham was at the far end of the bar, and I was serving down this end."

"He got pretty angry, did Bellingham."

"That's as maybe."

"Went red, like he was going to choke."

"He often does. It's blood pressure."

"Like I said, it's something you should tell the police."

Stan Podmore shook his head contemptuously.

"What you don't realize, Jim, is that the police and publicans are natural enemies. You can suck up to them any amount of times, but come the crunch they're your enemies still. I'll tell them if they ask, and that's all I'll do. Nick Bellingham may be a foreigner, but he drinks double Scotches when he's in funds. Show me a policeman as does that and happen I'll go volunteering information to him. Not before."

When she had fed her children, home from school, fielded their questions about the murder, told them of the visit of the two policemen, adjudicated in their quarrels, supervised their television watching, boiled milk for their good-night drinks and got them off to bed, Molly Kegan went around the house doing all the necessary late-night things. Then she took herself off to her lonely bedroom, where she wept herself to sleep, grieving for the only person in her life with wit and strength of purpose, the only woman she had known who had shown her there was something better than the life of drudgery and limited horizons that was what she had known since her marriage. In this house Lydia was mourned.

And thousands of miles away, at a sparsely attended press conference, the topic of Lydia Perceval's death surfaced too. Robert Loxton presided, with practised good-humour. His expedition had tested U.S. Army survival kit and rations during a four months period, winter to summer, on Mount McKinley. Interest had been high when he gave a press conference in Anchorage, but then there isn't a great deal of interest going on in Alaska. Here the reporters were bored, and were only interested in getting quotable quotes about the survival rations, which had come in for a great deal of criticism from American servicemen during the Gulf War.

"The curry was diabolical," said Loxton obligingly. "Like stewed Indian socks. On the other hand the goulash was palatable, and we found the dehydrated orange juice a real life-saver."

"You look pretty fit," drawled one reporter.

"Of course I'm fit. I've been doing this sort of expedition all my life. And I hope to go on doing them for a while yet."

The next question came out of the blue.

"Lydia Perceval was your aunt, wasn't she?" asked a young reporter.

Robert Loxton's brow creased.

"Lydia Perceval is my cousin. . . . What do you mean *was?*"

"Came through on the line a few hours ago. She's dead. Been murdered."

"*Murdered?* . . . You're not serious?"

Several men in the Defense Department room nodded.

"Found murdered in Yorkshire, England," said one.

"The obits will be in tomorrow's papers," put in another. "Her books were very well thought of in this country."

Robert Loxton's face crumpled, and he

looked down at the table for a few moments.

"Sorry," he said, looking up again. "It's a bit of a shock. Lydia was a friend as well as a relation. If there are no more questions. . . ."

CHAPTER 13

The signpost that said Fieldhay Farm was very old, its wood cracked, but someone had painted over the letters so that they were easily legible. Charlie swung the car into the lane, and they bumped and swayed their way along to the farmhouse. It was a smallish, rickety structure that did not look as if it had ever housed prosperity. They got out and stretched their legs, Charlie feeling like an alien intruder. Mike Oddie went up to the door and banged with the hefty iron knocker. Inside all was silence. They peered through the window of the sitting room.

"Cheerier inside than out," commented Mike.

They went round to the back of the farm. Hens scratching around in a coop, grunts from a sty some way away. It was a dirty, disorderly, healthy scene, though Charlie Peace thought the smell was something he would not care to get used to.

"Your eyes must be better than mine," said Mike. "Can you see him anywhere?"

Charlie jumped on an oil drum near the back door of the farm, and scanned the landscape.

Rolling green hills in a summer haze. The nearest village, he estimated, must be all of five miles away. Eerie. He concentrated on nearer at hand.

"There's a moving speck on a field over there," he said, pointing to his left. "If that's still Fieldhay Farm that will probably be our man. But it's ten minutes' walk away."

"Then we walk," said Mike, setting out along a well-defined path. "Don't you Londoners ever walk?"

Charlie sighed, jumped off the drum, and followed him.

"'Course we do. From the pub to the Underground. And often just changing lines involves a hell of a hike. If it wasn't for the buskers we'd go mad with boredom."

When they had got a fair way Mike Oddie registered the speck working in the field, then registered that the speck had straightened and was watching their approach.

"Well, at least he isn't going and lying on the sacrificial slab like Tess of the D'Urbervilles," he said. Charlie raised his eyebrows.

"What on earth put Tess of the D'Urbervilles into your head, sir?"

"Oh, I don't know: farms, fields, backbreaking work."

"Yeah, I saw the film. Tess didn't have a beard though . . . Oh! Neither does this bloke."

The man coming towards them was indeed clean-shaven.

"But it seems this is our man," said Mike. "And apparently he knows who we are."

He was wearing an old khaki shirt, decidedly dirty trousers and boots. His body was sliding into plumpness, and his hairline was receding, but it was an open, attractive face. He was fairly tall, but would he seem to a youngster to be fit, Charlie wondered? Perhaps to Jason Wetherby, he concluded. And he suspected that hard, physical work was getting him into the sort of shape he would not have been in a year or two back. He had been harvesting carrots, and Charlie could see them lying in cases. Jamie Loxton could hardly be blamed for the carrots, which must have been sown by someone else, but still Charlie registered that, like most organic produce he had ever seen, they looked knobbly, meagre and dirty. He didn't doubt that they were chock-a-block full of all sorts of things that gave an added zing to life, but aesthetically he preferred the supermarket variety. The man was now upon them, smiling, hand outstretched.

"I'm Jamie Loxton, brother of the more famous Robert," he said with a grin. "You must be the policemen."

"I'm Detective Superintendent Oddie. This

is Detective Constable Peace. You were expecting us?"

He nodded, the frank smile still on his face.

"Of course. Someone will have told you that Lydia's ex was back in the area. I should think you already know that I went to see her a couple of weeks ago. Now" — he looked around him, sizing things up — "how shall we organise this? Do we need to go back to the house?"

"Not at all," said Mike. "We don't want to keep you from your work longer than necessary."

"Right." Jamie Loxton upended a case and took it over towards the walled border of the field. "I'm quite happy with this, if you two can take the wall."

It was Charlie Peace's first experience of dry-stone walling as a perch. It was cold, hard, but a solid base. He took out his notebook as Mike Oddie began his questioning.

"To get the obvious point out of the way first: what were you doing on Monday night?"

"Right. Mary and I discussed that —"

"You did?"

"Naturally we did. I may be 'unsatisfactory,' you know, but you mustn't think I'm completely stupid. My ex-wife is killed shortly after I return to the district — of course you're going to be interested in me, and what I was doing when she was killed."

"Fair enough. So what were you doing?"

"From about a quarter to eight until about half past nine we were in the White Rose restaurant at Luddenden."

"That's one of a chain, isn't it — attached to the Micklethwaite brewery pubs?"

"That's right. I drove from there to Kedgely, and dropped Mary off outside her post office shop at ten to ten — she saw it by the chapel clock, which is very reliable, she says. She thinks other people may have seen us too. They're a nosey lot in Kedgely, and there was still a bit of light."

Mike Oddie had been doing some calculations.

"Bly is — what? — ten to fifteen minutes from here?"

"Easily fifteen in my car, and along those roads," said Jamie Loxton. "If you're toying with the idea I could do it in under ten, try doing it yourself. I take it village gossip is correct, and Lydia was killed around ten?"

"I didn't say that. Any back-up to your account of when you left the restaurant?"

Loxton smiled.

"Mary thinks the staff may remember. We were the last to leave, and they were willing us to go. Monday night's hardly lively in a place like that. Then after we'd paid the bill

I couldn't find my car keys, and I got into a great flap. Typical Loxton cock-up — but I love Muriel, my old Volksie, and I didn't want to leave her in their car park overnight. It's the sort of car young layabouts think they have a right to commandeer and crash."

"I had a meal in a White Rose restaurant the other night," put in Charlie. "Army surplus steaks and soggy vegetables. But the chit when I paid had the time on it. Probably that's standard equipment throughout the chain."

He launched at Jamie Loxton one of his ferocious smiles, but Jamie just nodded calmly.

"Good. That'll be the best confirmation."

"And after you dropped your girlfriend off?" Mike asked.

"Drove straight here, did one or two late-night things around the farm, then went to bed. I can't imagine there will be anyone to confirm any of that." He gestured around with his hand at the rolling landscape. "Nothing here to observe me — just the odd crow having a sleepless night."

"Right. Well, I think that covers all we need to know about Monday night." Mike Oddie observed his man, still sitting as relaxedly as was possible on the upturned wooden crate. "Let's get on to other things. Why did you come back to this district, sir?"

Jamie Loxton grinned.

"Easy. My girlfriend has kept the shop in Kedgely for the past year. Escapee from chronic overwork, due to government cuts in grants to local authorities. I was looking for a farm, so I looked in this area."

"It didn't bother you, that you would be coming back to live near your ex-wife?"

"It didn't bother *me*. I went to see her, and she said it didn't bother her. I'm a Yorkshire-man, and I know this part of Yorkshire well, from childhood visits. It's a perfectly natural place for me to settle."

"And you had lived with your wife in Bly while you were married?"

"Nearby, but very briefly. We had a tiny flat in London while I had my job in the City. When I lost it her parents let us live in an equally tiny cottage they owned near Bly. While I was 'finding my feet,' they said. It soon became obvious that Lydia did not be-lieve I ever would find my feet. She certainly made it clear that she wasn't going to help in the search. She suggested over supper one evening that the marriage wasn't working, and I obliged her by moving out."

"I see . . . What kind of marriage was it, sir?"

"Short."

"You think she needed a . . . stronger per-sonality as a husband?" Jamie grimaced.

"The received wisdom then was that she married me because she couldn't get Robert, my brother. There may be something in that. Certainly it's true that she liked decisive men, who knew what they wanted and went after it."

Mike Oddie nodded, and looked at Charlie.

"Yes, that was rather our impression of her. And on your side, sir?"

Jamie frowned, and for the first time looked uncertain.

"You mean why did I marry her? That's a tough one . . . I suppose I sort of fell into it, like I've fallen into most things in my life. She was always so bright and funny and determined as a child — really a vibrant personality. There was a will of iron there too, but I don't know if I understood that. Perhaps I did, and thought that was what I needed. But it didn't work out like that. She didn't transfer some of her strong will to me. She just made me feel inadequate. Lydia was good at making people feel inadequate."

"You say it was short," Oddie said. "How long?"

"Just a few months. It's all a bit of a haze, really — from being in a clinch with her on a river-boat going up the Thames, to marrying her in a Registry Office, to being shown the door. *She* married *me* — and then unmarried herself. I don't, to be honest, remember all that much about being married to her, and I suspect Lydia would have said the same. A piece of adolescent folly."

"When was this, sir?"

"Oh . . . nineteen fifty-nine. Thea was breast-feeding Maurice, I remember, and Gavin was already chattering brightly. At the time I wondered whether Lydia had married me because she wanted a child. If so she soon decided she didn't want one by me."

"And that — the few months' marriage — was the end of all connection with Lydia?"

"Absolutely," said Loxton, with a decisive nod of the head. "I occasionally heard about her from my parents. Read one of her books once — rather good, though not my sort of thing. I like thrillers, when I read at all. Yes, that was it."

"Except that you went to see her a couple of weeks ago."

"Oh yes. Right. Thought it would be the done thing, under the circumstances."

"And how . . . how did the meeting go?"

"Perfectly well. . . ." Jamie Loxton suddenly decided on honesty. He grinned again. "Well, a bit frostily, I suppose. Once she had wiped you off her slate, Lydia really didn't want you popping up on that slate again. If she decided you'd never amount to anything, then she didn't want you to get *anything* right. But we kept up appearances, talked for — what? — a quarter of an hour, said unfond farewells, and I took my leave."

"There was no row?"

"No row."

"We hear that Mrs Perceval was . . . rather upset after you left. Threw things around, and so on."

His eyebrows flew up in genuine surprise.

"Really? Good Lord! I wouldn't have thought she'd consider me worth getting angry about. I'm flattered, in a way."

"That you . . . made an impression?"

"Yes. Not much got through to Lydia emotionally, you know. I've always had the impression she regarded me as roughly on the level of the common caterpillar."

Oddie shifted his buttocks on his chilly perch, and Charlie did the same.

"You've had rather a . . . varied career, haven't you, sir?" Oddie asked.

"Chequered is the word you want, Superintendent. No need to aim at tactfulness with me. I've gone from job to job, expedient to expedient. Everybody likes me, nobody thinks I'm up to much. I've sold everything from *Encyclopaedia Britannica*s to Christmas wrapping paper. I've worked in national government, local government, British Rail, a pawnbroker's in a back street in Bolton. I've wielded a pick on the roads, I've carried a hod on a building site, I've worked in a travel agent's, which was perhaps the worst of all. You name it, I've done it."

"All perfectly legal occupations."

"All perfectly legal. If you're asking if I have a record —"

"I'm not. I know you haven't. Of course you were questioned by police about —"

Jamie Loxton put up his hand.

"Spare me! I know what I was questioned by police about. I'd be willing to admit that now and then I've been lucky. That questions could have been asked that I wouldn't have been able to wriggle out of. In fact, generally speaking I've been lucky. I've seldom gone hungry, usually had friends to help me out of scrapes, and my family were bricks. I'm like a slice of bread that somehow lands buttered side up every time."

"And now you've got a regular girlfriend and a farm of your own."

Jamie looked up at him with that expression of guileless amiability that must have won him numberless floats from casual acquaintances in bars and clubs.

"Exactly. You're asking how it came about, are you?"

"Well, there does seem to have been some

215

transformation in your fortunes," Oddie suggested. "One might say a transformation in your character."

"Fair enough. No one's more conscious of that than I am. The love of a good woman, I suppose you'd say. Mary's a cracker — a rock. The sort of support, you might say, that Lydia could have been, but wasn't."

"How long have you known her?"

"Just a year. That was the anniversary we were celebrating on Monday. We met in a pub in Sowerby Bridge. She'd been finalising arrangements to take over the shop and post office here, and I'd been looking at a farm near Halifax. We clicked. Then this farm came on the market. One day I hope she'll marry me. End of fairy story in which the frog becomes the handsome prince. Only I never was repulsively froggy, I hope, and I'm a very middle-aged prince."

There was still something that puzzled Oddie.

"Buying this farm, sir: I don't get the feeling you've been very flush with money in the past. . . ."

"Oh, that's easy. No mystery about that. My parents died — my mother about four years ago, my father eighteen months ago. They left everything to me."

Charlie put in: "Isn't that a bit surprising?"

216

"Frankly I was flabbergasted." Jamie Loxton turned his ingenuous gaze in his direction. "They hadn't told me, you see, in case I started trading on my 'great expectations.' They knew me."

"But why? —"

"Why throw good money down such a gaping hole? Well, they were very remarkable people — not at all the caricature North Country businessmen you get in television plays. They were open-minded, intelligent people. They loved and admired Robert, supported his ventures and schemes early on. But over the years they came to the conclusion that he'd gone on with them altogether too long — lived in a sort of perpetual adventure novel. And they knew he was a manager and a survivor: he'd go on doing what he wanted, and raising the money for it, whatever they did. If he got the cash they knew he'd blow it on one spectacular trek across the Gobi Desert, or whatever. They exercised their option to say that wasn't what they wanted their money to go on, and preferred to give the lot to me. It was to provide one last, really good chance of making good. I don't mean it was a fortune, but the sum I inherited does mean that I can make losses on this place for quite a number of years and not go under."

"Wasn't your brother shat off about that?"

Charlie asked. Jamie Loxton shook his head.

"He was very good about it. He'd been consulted years before — either by letter, or when he visited my parents, which wasn't very often. He wrote to me from some god-forsaken hole when he heard Father was dead. Said he'd known about it for years, congratulated me, said he understood why they did it. I remember he wrote: 'It will enable you to settle down in comfort, if that's what you want, or blow it all gloriously if you prefer.' I suspect he'd have thought better of me if I'd blown it. I guess that what he *thought* would happen would be that I'd let it slip through my fingers somehow or other. Anyway, now he'll be able to make his own choices with Lydia's money. He'll blow it gloriously, I'm sure. Siberia or the Kalahari Desert will be the gainers."

"He knew he was her heir?" Oddie asked.

"Oh yes, I think so. Maybe I shouldn't say that?" He looked anxiously from face to face.

"He was an awfully long way away at the time," said Oddie. Jamie relaxed.

"That's right. Well yes, she did tell him. I expect it was originally Gavin and Maurice — in fact I'm quite sure it was. Then, when Gavin was dead and Maurice disappointed her — something Lydia never forgave — she changed her will entirely to leave it to Robert.

As I said, the received idea when they were young was that she loved him."

"But it was not returned?"

"Robert has casual women, never just one woman."

"And he told you he knew?"

"My father did. Mentioned several times that Robert knew he would get the bulk of Lydia's estate. Maybe Dad was trying to justify what they'd done, without actually telling me. Because there was no guarantee that Lydia would die first."

"Right," said Oddie. "I don't think there's anything else for the moment. All the stuff about your movements will have to be checked, of course." He turned to Charlie enquiringly. "Is there anything I've forgotten?"

Charlie smiled his intimidating smile at Jamie Loxton.

"Your beard, sir: when did you shave it off?"

Loxton's expression was one of amused surprise.

"My beard? What on earth has that to do with anything? Oh, let me see: several days ago. Sunday, I think. Yes, I rather think I've shaved four mornings now."

"I see. . . . So you would have been clean-shaven when you were at the White Rose on Monday night?"

"Oh yes. And probably looking a bit odd,

too: part brown, part white. It's getting a bit more even now."

"Why did you shave it off?" Mike asked.

"Difficult to say," said Jamie, hardly taking the question seriously. "It had come to seem like a prop. Designed to give me the sort of feeling American men get from carrying a gun. I didn't need it anymore . . . I seem to remember Lydia being sarcastic on the subject."

"Well, I think that's it. We'll be back to you if necessary."

The two men jumped gratefully off the wall, dusted down their backsides, shook hands with Jamie Loxton, and began the trudge back to their car. When Charlie turned his head Jamie was already bent over his carrots, his face hidden.

"First impressions?" Oddie asked.

"I liked him. But then, as he said, people do like him, and I can believe that. That could be a dangerous position to be in — or at least, it could put you in the way of pretty powerful temptations. . . . But that wasn't what you wanted, was it?"

"Not really, though I agree, for what it's worth. First impressions of what he said was what I was after. Did it make sense, did you believe him?"

Charlie had thought about it, and replied at once.

"The *first* thing he said to us was 'brother of the more famous Robert.' The last thing he said was something about Lydia making sarcastic remarks about his beard. You wonder whether he is quite the changed character he thinks he is."

"Defines himself in terms of other people?" Charlie grinned.

"That sounds like psychologists' jargon to me. Let's say he's very lacking in self-confidence, self-trust."

"Maybe. But regaining confidence must be a gradual process, after all those years of being an unsatisfactory blob whom people shook their heads over. Anyway, it's never easy being the relation of a famous person. Think of being Dickens's brother. Or Margaret Thatcher's sister. Anything else?"

"The meal at the White Rose. That's the crux, isn't it? If he was there at around nine thirty, and letting his fiancée out of the car at ten to ten, then he can't have been the man in the wood the boy saw, beard or no beard. And I don't see he can be whoever interrupted Lydia's phone call just before ten."

"So, subject to checking, you'd rule him out?"

Charlie thought.

"Only if we make the assumption that the person who interrupted her phone call then strangled her."

"Good man," said Oddie approvingly. "And that seems a probability, but it's far from a fact. Anything else?"

"Obviously we'd like to know if Robert Loxton really took his being cut out of his parents' will in the relaxed way his brother said he did. Must be a bit of a saint."

"Or someone who isn't primarily interested in money."

"He seems to have spent a lot of his life raising it," Charlie pointed out. "Then I wasn't too happy about all that business of mislaying his keys at the White Rose. Too coincidental. Too much like a ploy to make sure he was remembered."

"You speak like a man who has never lost his car keys in his life."

"Can't recall that I have. I've had them nicked."

"There is a sort of person who puts his glasses down somewhere and goes all round the house looking for them later, and there's also the sort who never does. I'd have put this chap down as the first sort, just on his life record. Most probably his brother is just as definitely in the second category. . . . Here we are. I'll just get on to Halifax and see if anything has come up."

As they started the car and began down the

lane to the road Oddie got the message from Halifax that Robert Loxton had heard of his cousin's murder in Washington, had flown home overnight, and had contacted the Halifax police from Heathrow. He was on his way north in a hired car, and would meet Oddie at his cousin's cottage some time between two and three, if there were no major hold-ups on the M1.

"Splendid!" said Oddie, as Charlie emerged onto the winding little country road. "I have the feeling that if anyone knew and understood Lydia Perceval it was the more famous Robert."

CHAPTER 14

There was a brisk wind, and puffy clouds were scudding across the sky when they arrived back at the cottage, giving it a more romantic appearance than the rich, classical complacence it had worn when they had first seen it. Both images, Oddie thought, were deceptive. And so was the image Lydia presented to the world.

Reporters had lingered around the cottage for several hours after Lydia's murder, but when they found there was nothing but policemen to see they had drifted off down the hill in search of refreshment, and by now most of them had left the village entirely. There was still a constable guarding the cottage — a fresh-faced and freckled young man called Holdsworth, of about Charlie's age. He led them through to the study.

"I've been looking through the books," he explained. "Hoping to find some old letters used as a bookmark. No luck. She mostly used bits torn off a pad, and old bills. From the bills it looks as if she got most things delivered — meat, bread, drink. Then she made occasional visits to a supermarket in Halifax and really stocked up, including stuff for the freezer."

"Supermarket bills are very informative these days," said Oddie, peering at some of them. "One day they'll be a great help on a case, but I can't see that this will be the one."

"One thing I did find was the appointments book," said the young constable. He leaned forwards and took it from a row of books behind the typewriter on Lydia's desk. "It's a National Gallery one, with pictures, and it looks like any other book."

"Good work," said Oddie. "Something we missed." He turned to July, and to Monday the twelfth. Charlie looked over his shoulder as he pointed to the entry: "Boston Spa. Oliver Marwick 5 P.M."

"That's what they call negative evidence," Oddie said. "That's to say, no bloody evidence at all."

"We never thought the chap murdered her by appointment," Charlie pointed out. "All the evidence points to his having got in while she was down in the village, perhaps using his own key, then surprised her when she was on the phone and strangled her."

"Yes," said Mike, flicking through the pages. "So long as we don't *assume* that's what happened. . . . Not much here. Maybe because she was writing the book. 'Tea Ted and Colin.' 'Tea Maurice.' She puts 'The boys' the first couple of days when they started coming up regularly, then didn't bother any longer. The story of a successful take-over."

"Are you happy with Lydia's last words?" Charlie asked suddenly.

Oddie swung round. Charlie's question chimed in with a niggling doubt which had been rattling around in the back of his own mind and refusing to come forward.

"Her last words?"

"As Marwick remembers them: 'What's that?' 'But' and 'Rob.' The last with a sort of questioning sound, you said. We've been taking it that she was surprised by a noise, was puzzled because there should have been no one in the house, that she started to say 'robbers,' and then was strangled."

"Actually I'm keeping a more open mind than that, but what's wrong with that as a possible scenario?"

"Nobody uses the word 'robbers' anymore," said Charlie. "She would have said 'burglars,' or 'housebreakers.' If it was outside it would be 'muggers.' 'Robbers' has an old-fashioned sound to it, like highway robbers. I'd say the only time it's used these days is when we talk of 'bank-robbers,' and even then people are starting to say 'bank raiders'."

"Hmmm. You've got a point. But you've got to remember that Lydia Perceval *was* an old-fashioned person, and one who professionally lived in the past. In that solicitor's file there were various copies of letters, and she usually signed off 'Yours sincerely.' Not many people do that these days, apart from old people. Also, this was heard over a telephone line, at a moment of great stress. It could be almost any word. But what was your idea?"

"That there was someone hiding behind the door there, perhaps not expecting her to come into the study at that time of night. If she was standing in the way her body suggested she would surely have caught a glimpse of whoever it was coming towards her."

"And?"

"And if she knew him she wouldn't say 'robbers,' she'd say his name . . . Robert, for example."

"But that's —" Mike Oddie began, then stopped. "Well, no, not impossible. Unlikely, but not impossible. Something that we'll have to look into."

"He's the main beneficiary," Charlie pointed out. "A man who's spent his life getting together money for expeditions, treks, survival schemes."

"All right, all right. Point taken. But remember, Oliver Marwick said there was a sort of question in the way she said it."

"I know. As if she was sort of bewildered. So maybe someone who looked like Robert, but who she realised wasn't."

"Could be. Another possibility. Let's not get ourselves into any preconceived position before he arrives."

"Fine by me," said Charlie amiably. "Let's talk about the weather. Or the Yorkshire Cricket Club. Why are people at the Yorkshire Cricket Club always screaming and fighting each other?"

"Ask me again when we have the whole evening. It's a bit like the Church of England: it all goes back a long way, and has something to do with theology. Ah now — is this our man?"

A blue car had drawn up in the opening outside the cottage gates. A man got out, opened the gate, closed it carefully, then strode towards the cottage. The impression that this was a young man came from his extreme leanness, and his general air of being in excellent condition.

"Let him in," said Mike Oddie to Holdsworth. "Then you can scoot off for an hour or two."

When Robert Loxton was shown in Charlie could see that the air of youth was deceptive.

The dark hair was streaked with grey, there were wrinkles gathering about the eyes, and the neck was becoming scraggy in that tell-tale way that always marks out ageing people who have hitherto had an air of youth. A very vital, energetic, impressive figure none the less. And one, Charlie noted from the concentration of tan around the nose, eyes and forehead, and lack of it around the chin and cheeks, who had recently shaved off a beard. But that was only to be expected, of course, in one who had recently emerged from four months in the wilds of Alaska.

"Robert Loxton," he said, coming forward and shaking hands with both of them. "This is a dreadful business. I heard it in Washington. At a press conference — the damnedest way to hear. I flew straight here."

Oddie introduced himself and Charlie, and gestured to a chair.

"No thanks. I've been sitting on a plane, sitting in the driving seat of a car." He began striding up and down the small study. Charlie felt that any room would seem too small for him, and that perhaps this was an impression he liked to give. "Was it here that it was done?"

"Yes," said Oddie, feeling it was Loxton who was commanding the situation rather than himself, but deciding to leave it that way for a bit. "She was on the telephone, or so we think."

"Poor Lydia. What a damned . . . inappropriate way to go."

"Yes." Oddie nodded his agreement. "We have the impression of a well-organised, rather conservative, rather cool lady — would you agree with that?"

"I think so. If you're talking about the Lydia of today — or rather yesterday." He grinned suddenly, revealing brilliant, even teeth. "Lydia and I once 'had something going,' as they say these days. She wasn't so cool then."

"What went wrong?"

"Nothing exactly went wrong. We just had different ideas. To slide from one cliché to another: she wanted greater commitment than I was willing to give. Or, as we would have put it, she stuck out for marriage and I wasn't interested in that. She went off and married my brother Jamie, and that *was* a disaster. That, I suppose, was the basis of Lydia's coolness."

"But you remained fond of her?"

"Oh immensely. We didn't see each other often —"

"How often?"

"I suppose every year or two, though sometimes it could go longer than that. It rather depended on how long I had between expeditions, and whether I was raising money in this country or abroad. But we'd try and meet up, generally in London, and if we couldn't we'd have a long natter on the phone."

"And of course she made you her heir."

"Yes. Not very long after Gavin died."

"And you knew this?"

"Oh yes. She told me. I didn't tell anyone much, but I'm pretty sure I told my father. It was always a long shot — likely to come to me, if at all, long after I could put it to any good use."

"You mention meeting in London. Did you often come here? Did you have a key?"

"Good Lord, no. I've only been here once — no, twice — in my life. Last time was — oh, about six or seven years ago, when I happened to be in Leeds. That was too soon after Gavin's death to be a really happy occasion. . . . So you think whoever did it may have had a key, do you? That should narrow the field a bit. But I'm afraid I've never had one. And I very much doubt whether Jamie had one either."

"Oh?"

"It was several years after the marriage that Lydia bought this place."

"Why do you mention your brother?" Charlie asked.

"Well, I imagined you'd be looking at him

— ex-husband and all that."

"You knew he was back in the district?"

"Is he? No, I didn't, actually." He patted his jacket. "I've got a letter from him somewhere, but I haven't got around to reading it. I must say, quite apart from the key, there's no way I can see my kid brother committing murder."

"He seems, in fact, to have a pretty good alibi," said Oddie. "Though we're not one hundred per cent sure about the time of the murder. Of course his involvement with Lydia Perceval was very early on, like your own. You must have noticed changes in her over the years, sir."

"Yes . . . Yes, I suppose I did. Seeing her at intervals, sometimes long intervals, one did notice the way she was changing." He came to rest by the desk, and sat on it, looking at the policemen straight. "I should say that I always thought Lydia a very remarkable person. She knew what she wanted and she went for it. I like that. Notice that all the early books were of popular figures — Nelson, Lawrence of Arabia, people like that. Then when she had established herself, got a faithful readership, she could branch out on to less glamorous figures that she felt really needed treatment. Who was she writing about when she died?"

"Charles the tenth of France."

"There you are. Who's heard of him? But the book would have sold, because she'd built up a trusting readership in the course of her writing life, people who knew she would make the story interesting. Her *Byron* was one of the books we took with us to Mount McKinley: wonderfully entertaining. She liked men with a spark of the devil in them. She also liked achievers, as you may have guessed. I remember once suggesting to her that she do Scott of the Antarctic, and she waved a hand in the way she had and said that heroic failures were for other people: the British loved them but she didn't. . . . What I'm saying is that I admired her, but that there were one or two negative aspects that emerged over the years."

"In particular?"

Robert Loxton had resumed his energetic march around the study, and now stopped by the door.

"I was always a bit dubious about her attitude to people. I sometimes wondered — this may sound egotistical, chauvinistic, even — if it was the lack of a satisfying marriage that caused her to . . . use people. Quite unconsciously, and in the nicest possible way, she attached people to her, if she thought it worthwhile to. And she'd take them over and use them. If they became no longer useful to her, she'd detach herself, very kindly, very gradually. You'd hardly notice it, but you'd no longer be part of her world."

"Is that what happened with the nephews?"

"Maurice and Gavin? Partly. But it was more complex than that. There was genuine love there — especially with Gavin. Of course I only know about this from Lydia's point of view. I've very seldom met Andy and Thea in the last twenty or thirty years, and when I have it's been on a purely social level. But even just hearing about it from Lydia's point of view I could see the dangers."

"What were they, do you think?"

"She loved them, but she was using them too — to live out her own dreams and fantasies, to do some of the things she couldn't do but would have loved to do. There is a sort of inbuilt irony about being a *writer* who deals with heroic and glamorous or even grandly sinful figures, isn't there? So Gavin was to be the glamorous serviceman, and Maurice was to save the country politically."

"Ah — we hadn't heard that."

"This was in the seventies, when politically everything was a bit tatty and unsatisfactory. When the Conservative Party was taken over by yuppies whose idea of glory was a windfall killing on the stock exchange she lost interest. Recently she'd just waved politics aside — something beneath serious attention. But at one time Maurice was to be the nation's saviour. I don't think that ambition lasted very long. By all accounts she got Maurice wrong."

"Oh?" said Charlie. "What sort of a person is he?"

"I don't know, to be honest, what he *is*. But as a boy he seemed likely to grow up into rather a quiet figure: more Geoffrey Howe than Michael Heseltine. Anyway, from what I hear when he grew up he just went his own way. And Lydia simply moved him out of her life. But by then the damage was done."

"Damage? To Maurice?"

"Maybe. I hardly know the man, as I said, though I believe he's doing rather well in television. No — I was thinking about Andy and Thea. When Lydia took over somebody she hardly left room for anybody else. I tried to warn her, but in emotional matters Lydia could only see one viewpoint. Andy and Thea lost their sons, at least for a time . . . and one of them they lost for good."

"You . . . you think they hated her?"

"I don't know. But I know how I'd feel."

"Yes. . . ." Mike Oddie thought. "In fact there's been a more recent case of Mrs Perceval moving in on other people's lives."

"Oh?"

"Two boys again. In the last few weeks of her life."

"And how did the parents feel about that?"

"The mother's very sick, which obviously helped the process on. The father was apparently delighted. Took the burden off his shoulders when the mother went into hospital. He gives the impression of not being a particularly perceptive man — unless he's having us on. In any case the process was in its early days. No doubt it took a while until the Hoddles realized what was happening, and they seem very much brighter."

"I remember the Hoddles as a very nice couple." He ceased abruptly from ranging up and down the room and sat down: long, lean, full of life and vitality. "Thinking back on what I've said, I may have been a bit hard on Lydia. I suppose when you find out someone's been murdered you inevitably cast around for reasons. Lydia was a fine historian, a splendid writer; she was fun to be with, and good to be seen with. Her opinions were sensible, and she argued them well. I was always happy when we were going to have dinner together, and if I was uncertain about anything I'd always listen to what she had to say on the subject. I've no evidence that Thea and Andy resented her influence on their boys, and it sounds as if Maurice came to no permanent harm. If you could tell me she might have been killed by the good old passing vagrant or in the course of a house-breaking that's the explanation I'd plump for."

"It's still a possibility," said Oddie neutrally. "But a shooting in the course of a break-in is a good deal more likely than a strangling. I don't suppose you'd be any good at identifying anything that's missing, sir?"

"No use at all." He looked round. "Nice place, nice furniture, a good feel to the place. But I remember practically nothing from my previous visits."

"What will you do with it?"

"Put it on the market, or let it until the market perks up. Not a time for selling houses at the moment. I'm not the settling-down type, and when I'm forced into it it certainly won't be in somewhere like Bly. I suppose there's a pub in the place that takes visitors, is there? I don't fancy sleeping in this place, and it doesn't seem fair to plonk myself on Jamie, wherever he is."

"Yes, there's a pub just down the hill. Purely as a formality, sir, could you tell me what you were doing at the time of the murder?"

"Sure. You tell me the time of the murder."

"Say — it's a distinct possibility — Monday at ten in the evening."

"Lord — what's the time difference between here and Anchorage? I came via Washington, so I'm not too sure."

Oddie leaned over to the desk and dialled 155.

"Nine hours behind GMT," he said when he came back to them. "That's ten because we're on Summer Time."

"Right. Midday, then. We had a press conference starting at ten. There was a lot of interest, and I remember looking at my watch at half past eleven, when it was still going on. I should think it broke up a bit before twelve."

"Right. You'd got back to Anchorage the day before, had you?"

"No, we got back on Friday. The weekend was a bad time for a press conference."

"And you were staying? —"

"Officially at the Hilton. In fact there are certain . . . needs, that are not catered for by U.S. Army emergency rations." He grinned. "Would you like her name and address?"

"Please."

He took out a pen and notebook and wrote it down rapidly.

"The phone number is from memory, but I think it's right. It's a girl I teamed up with when we were making all the preparations.

Girls are hard to come by in Anchorage, so I made a date for when the four months were up. I went to the Hilton every day to collect messages, but most of the time I was with her."

"And later?"

"Monday night I was with her. Then I took a late-night flight to Washington."

"Well, I think that will be enough, sir. Keep us informed where you are, will you? We'd rather you stayed in the area for a few days. Mrs Perceval's solicitors are Marwick, Chester and Jones, in Halifax. I imagine we'll be releasing the body fairly soon, so it should be possible to have the funeral next week."

Robert Loxton banged his forehead.

"Oh God — the funeral! I suppose I'll be expected to go. I didn't even get to my own parents' funerals, but since I'm the heir, and since I'm in this country. . . . Oh well, I'd better buy me a black tie."

"Did you resent your parents leaving everything to your brother, sir?" asked Oddie, looking straight at him as he stood by the door preparing to leave.

"No, I did not." He looked back at him, eyes sparkling in lean cheeks. "It was done after consultation with me. I've never had much difficulty raising money for what I want to do. They'd rather lost sympathy — or maybe just interest — over the years. So they wanted to leave it to Jamie as one last chance to settle down. I said: Right-ho. Go ahead. I may say I never thought it would become a police matter. And it's not really, is it?"

"Not so far as I know, sir. We won't keep you."

Robert Loxton smiled briefly and strode out to his car. They watched him through the window. Oddie turned to Charlie.

"Well?"

"I bet if you phoned that number you'd get his woman friend."

Oddie raised his eyebrow.

"Meaning?"

"It was all too pat."

"He'd had her number with him four long months on Mount McKinley," Oddie pointed out.

"He doesn't strike me as the type to moon over a telephone number in the frozen wastes. But what I meant was, it was all too pat, down to the supposed uncertainty about the number. He knew the number perfectly well."

"Yes . . . I think, you know, that when the crime is murder people begin acting from the moment that they hear about it. People close to the victim, even people quite distant as well. Perhaps it dates back to hanging, I don't know. But as soon as he heard this chap probably said to himself: 'When did it happen? Over the weekend I've got Karen Paulson to vouch for me. Then I gave a press conference, then I flew to Washington. . . ." And so on. It doesn't mean he's implicated in any way. Everyone will have done the same. And remember he's used to performing — for potential sponsors, in press conferences and so on."

"All the same," said Charlie, "I think you should ask the Anchorage police to check the girlfriend out. And ask them to check the time of the press conference and the date very carefully."

"I shall. Are there any other eggs you wish to teach me to suck?"

"No, grandma," said Charlie, grinning. "He's perfectly plausible and rather impressive, and you're probably right he can have nothing to do with it. Why did he mention his brother, though, when he says he had no idea he was back in the neighbourhood?"

"Yes, I wondered about that. You're suggesting he wanted to draw him to our attention, even cast suspicion in that direction?"

"Sounds rotten put like that. Maybe diffuse suspicion a bit. There was a lot of talk about the Hoddles resenting Lydia's role without apparently any real knowledge to back it up. . . ." Charlie turned from the window and wandered over to the wall by the door. "I keep thinking about this picture."

Oddie turned round and came over.

"The picture of George the Fifth and Nicholas the whatever-it-was?"

"Yes. Like as two peas, like I said. How alike do you think they'd have been if they'd shaved their beards off?"

CHAPTER 15

Charlie Peace felt like a schoolboy who has been given an unexpected holiday. He felt the same sense of limitless possibilities open before him, the same feeling that he must not throw them away by squandering the time on irrelevancies. Mike Oddie had told him he would be tied up for much of the day on routine jobs, and had a visit to Marwick, Chester and Jones lined up for the afternoon. Charlie was free to do what he liked in the way of checking things that bothered him, talking to people on the fringes of the case.

"But leave the Hoddles," Oddie said. "He won't be back from school until late afternoon, and we both of us should be there."

Charlie felt what sports writers call a surge of adrenalin. Co-operation, swapping of views, plans of campaign were all very well, but there is nothing quite like freedom.

Liberated at last from supervision, the first thing he did was pure self-indulgence. He went to the Halifax Library to find pictures of George V and Nicholas II without beards. This was not as easy as he had expected. The English king was the problem: he seemed to have been hirsute from puberty on. Finally a librarian found a book of photographs from the Victorian court, with Prince George shortly before he went to sea. There was, Charlie thought, no more than a vague family resemblance between him and his Russian cousin. The shape of the head was similar, the look of the forehead, but the lower part of the face showed them to be not particularly alike. It was the beards that made the resemblance.

Having satisfied himself on this, Charlie grinned self-deprecatingly at the thought of how short a distance it got him. Beyond the fact that Robert and Jamie Loxton, though very different when clean-shaven, might look very similar with beards, he had discovered nothing. And since both men seemed to have tight alibis, he had got nowhere. Except that there was a man with a beard somewhere in the case, and he needed to be either accounted for or eliminated. Were Jamie and Robert Loxton's alibis as tight as they seemed? He felt he might be thought by Oddie to have wasted time, and decided to punish himself with a morning of routine. Still, it would do no harm to start it in the village of Kedgely.

They had already established by a telephone call to the White Rose in Luddenden that the final eaters of dinner on Monday the twelfth paid their bill at 9:26. They had talked to one of the waiters who was on duty that night, and he remembered the fuss over the lost keys, which he thought took up a good three or four minutes after that. He described Jamie Loxton with a fair degree of accuracy. Still, Lydia was not killed until ten — and ten *at the earliest*. Charlie left his car in a pub yard at Kedgely, which was a village of fifteen or twenty houses along a very minor road. The houses were mostly of stone, poky but attractive. Charlie set out in the direction of the village shop along a pavement so narrow as to be useless. It was in such an environment that Charlie felt at his most alien — a feeling that could be pleasurable as well as unsettling. There was no one in the street, but when he reached the door of the village shop he could hear gossip going on inside. His appearance put a stop to that: the customer smiled nervously and retreated from the shop. Charlie Peace did tend to have that effect on people.

"You must be the policeman," said Mary Scully.

He didn't have to ask how she knew. Kedgely saw few black people, and Jamie would have told her already that one of the detectives investigating the murder was black. The whole of Kedgely would know that, and would most probably know by now that he was back. It would be that sort of place.

"Just checking," he said. "I'm sure you understand that we have to. Now, you left the restaurant about 9:29 or so."

"Golly," said Mary, impressed. "You know more about our movements than we do ourselves."

Charlie favoured her with one of his more approachable grins. He liked what he saw. She was a slim, wiry woman in her forties — active, down-to-earth, easy to get on with. Certainly not like any of the media stereotypes of the social worker: batty, bossy or meddling.

"You then drove straight back here?"

"Yes, not very fast. Jamie's car doesn't *do* very fast. We got back at ten to ten by the chapel clock."

"Anybody vouch for that?"

"I don't know. I've tried to keep off the subject in the shop, though it's not easy. But we are a very nosey bunch — I include myself, because I used to be a social worker, and I still like poking my nose in other people's affairs. I would guess that if you ask around someone will have seen us. They'll be interested in whether I sleep at the shop or at Jamie's. Try Mrs Formby in Willow Bank. She's a widow lady who tends to dart over to the window every time she hears voices or a car. If she wasn't in bed by then it's ten to one she saw us."

"And you did sleep in the shop that night, and Mr Loxton drove off towards the farm?"

"Yes — I waved him off in that direction, *not* the direction of Bly."

"But of course he has nothing to back him up on his movements after ten to ten."

"Nothing except his obvious unsuitability as a murderer. I should have thought even the police would have seen that as a killer Jamie is a non-starter."

"This is my third murder. I'm keeping an open mind. But I've known drug-pushers who were the nicest guys in the world — boys I'd be happy if my sister took up with."

He grinned, more ferociously this time, and while Mary was formulating the objection that it wasn't because Jamie was too nice that he was a non-starter but because, well — Charlie had wheeled around and left the shop.

Mrs Formby at Willow Bank was, as expected, a most obliging witness.

"Oh yes, I saw them come back. I was just passing the window when he let her out of the car . . . No, I couldn't see him very well, but I saw her, and of course I know the car. It was still light, you see, or not quite dark. It was ten to ten by the chapel clock, and I remember thinking: ten to ten and still a bit of light."

"Call that thought?" Charlie said to himself, but he smiled his thanks and went back to his car, lodging in the back of his mind the thought that she probably hadn't seen the driver of the car at all.

His next stop was the little wood just above Lydia's cottage. He drove there at a moderate speed for him, and timed himself: twenty minutes. Jamie Loxton (assuming it was him in the car at Kedgely) could have been around Lydia's cottage by about ten past ten. Which left unaccounted for the man in the woods around twenty past nine, and the man who — person who — interrupted Lydia's phone call. Charlie drove into the wood and left the car on the lane leading towards the gravel pit. Then he got out and looked around. Somewhere in the undergrowth Jason Wetherby and his girlfriend were petting when the car drove up. He looked at his wristwatch and set off briskly along the path, then down the road to the cottage. Eight minutes. That would get the mystery man on to the scene probably around the time Lydia and the boys had set off for the village. Perhaps he had watched them.

Charlie had now approached the cottage from a new angle, and once more he stopped to look around him. Jason and his girlfriend had gone their separate ways back to Bly, he by the road down the hill, she by a back path. There was a path along the hedge which skirted the small back garden of the cottage. Charlie began along it. It was broad to start with, twin-tracked, until it led into the cottage's garage. Then it narrowed to become a normal country path across a tract of barren hillside. Charlie started down it, but frowning to himself. If the man in the woods was nothing to do with Lydia's murder — say he was the fancy man of someone in the village whose husband was on nights — then this path left him quite as exposed as the road down the hill. He stopped and looked: he could be seen from the kitchens on a little estate of private houses built off the main street of Bly, as well as from most of the houses in that street. He spotted at least three people who were watching him intently now. It was still twilight at half past nine, when the man would have gone down. In fact, he would have been even more exposed on the path, because people who saw him would have wondered why he was taking the path rather than the road. On the other hand, if it was someone with legitimate business in Bly, one who took this short cut to a house at the end of the street, why leave his car in the wood rather than on the road? Why not drive all the way there?

Charlie continued on down the path, and

found that it came out just beside the meagre house of the Bellingham family. He turned and made his way thoughtfully back up the hill and to his car. Then he drove out again on to the road and down to the village. He left his car in the main street. No point in trying to hide the fact that he was back: he was too conspicuous for that, and the whole village had registered his first visit. He made his way to Molly Kegan's council house, and was pleased to find her in.

"Yes, I'm free today." She smiled sadly, ushering him in. "I would have been up at Lydia's . . . the Bellingham man has asked me to go there, but I'm still thinking about it."

Waiting to discover whether one of that family was involved, Charlie thought. He was pleased to see that her eyes were no longer red, and that she seemed to have regained some reserves of fight. He saw on the battered coffee-table by one of the armchairs a prospectus for the Open University.

"Taking up study?"

"Yes, maybe. I thought of the awful . . . the awful *gap* that Lydia's death leaves in my life — the total lack of stimulus. I thought this might help me to fill it, if they'll accept me. They're quite flexible, I believe. It seemed like a good way of ensuring, in a small way,

that her influence lives on. Not that I'll necessarily do History — there seem to be a lot
of interesting courses. . . . Was there something you wanted?"

"Yes. I thought you might be able to tell
me which of the ladies in the village is the
best gossip."

She looked at him pityingly.

"You're very young, aren't you?"

"No, as a matter of fact I'm not," said Charlie, offended.

"When you're a bit older you'll know that
the best gossips are always men. I think it's
to their credit: women are too interested in
themselves to be first-rate gossips. What's the
time? Twelve o'clock. Go along to The
Wheatsheaf and you'll find Jim Scattergood
nursing a half of bitter in a corner. He'll be
a hundred times more reliable than her in the
post office."

"Right," said Charlie, trusting her judgment. "I'll go and have a chat with him."

"Oh, and by the way, Stan Podmore the
licensee was heard to say the other day that
he'll tell the police something or other when
they start buying double whiskies like Nick
Bellingham."

"Thanks for telling me. I'm not into whisky,
but I'll order one of those non-alcoholic wines.
The profit margin on them is even steeper."

Charlie recognised Jim Scattergood the moment he walked into The Wheatsheaf. He was not an old man — sixty perhaps — but he had sharp eyes in sunken features. He was sitting by the fireplace as if it was winter. It was obviously his favoured position, his by right, and good both for seeing and hearing. Charlie's eyes met his, and he went over to him.

"What are you having? Another half?"

"Very kind. It's the Theakston Special."

Charlie ordered it, and a hideously expensive non-alcoholic wine, and told Stan Podmore to keep the change. When he took them over to the table by the fireplace Jim Scattergood had a smile playing around his thin lips.

"What do you want to know then, lad?"

Charlie asked, to test him: "Who's young Jason Wetherby's girlfriend?"

"Oh, that'd be Julie Holmroyd," said Jim immediately. "None of t'parents knows, because they don't keep a watch. They go up to t'woods for a bit of the usual. Were they up there on t'night of t'murder?"

"Never you mind."

"Any road, I think young Julie's losing interest. That young Bellingham is a lot better looking — and a lot brighter too."

"I see. . . . What is it that the landlord

could tell us but hasn't got around to telling us yet?"

"Oh that. Well, he says it's nothing, but I say every little thing's important in a murder case."

"You've been watching Poirot on Sunday nights."

"Never watch telly. It's got nothing on life, hasn't telly. Well, as I were saying it were only *words*. But I'd say young Hoddle were pretty worked up. *Intense* — that's the word I'd use."

"I see. And when was this?"

"Night of t'murder it were. That's why folk remembers it. Night of t'murder, around ten."

"Could you be more exact?"

"No, I couldn't. You don't keep looking at t'clock when you're enjoying a pint of ale, 'cept if it's near closing time."

"What exactly happened?"

"Well, Bellingham come in, and he were being a bit of a blabbermouth as usual. Folk here don't think a lot to him — he's a foreigner, from down South somewhere. He's just tolerated, like. Any road, he were standing over at t'bar — over there, far end — and going on about Mrs Perceval, what an interest she were tekking in his boys, the amount of work she were doing to stand in for their mother, and so on, and so on. Well, o' course, unbeknownst to him, young Hoddle had come in for a pint ten minutes or so before him, and were stood just feet away from him, down t'other end of t'bar. I reckon they didn't know each other be sight, Bellingham having only moved here a matter o' months sin'. Any road, young Maurice, after a minute or two, he went down to Bellingham's end of t'bar, and started talking to him in a low voice — quiet-like at first."

"But not after a time?"

"Well, Bellingham's a thick-skulled bloke. Kept repeating how good Lydia Perceval had been, what a weight she'd tekken off his shoulders, and all that. Any road, young Maurice were gettin' more and more worked up. Till finally . . . But you'd better ask Stan there what he said. He were closer than me."

"Right, I will. Did you live in Bly while the younger Hoddles were growing up?"

"Oh aye. Lived here all me life."

"Tell me about it — when I've got you another half."

When he came back with two glasses he asked: "How was Lydia Perceval seen in the village?"

Jim Scattergood drank, then wiped his lips.

"Aah! Rather like t'lady of t'manor. That were how she went on, in a way. 'Course o' late years we hardly saw her. Ten year sin' we had a butcher and a baker here in t'village, and she'd walk down and shop here. Now there's nothing but an itty-bitty general store an' one or two poncy antique shops and the like. She must ha' driven somewhere to shop. Any road, we seldom saw her. Boasted of her, now an' then, wi' strangers, but seldom saw her. Even ten, fifteen year ago, when the Hoddle boys were growing up, what we saw were the boys going up *there*."

"So there wasn't a lot of toing and froing between the adult members of the family?"

"Happen there may have been once. Years and years before, when t'boys were little. Holidays abroad an' suchlike. But then Mrs Perceval became — well, almost famous, and very busy. And then t'boys started going up there. Every day it would be home from school then straight up to Aunt Lydia's. Sometimes they'd eat up there, sometimes they come home, but every day they'd go up there."

"What did the Hoddles think about it?"

"What do you suppose they thought? They said nowt, neither Thea nor Andy. But it were like it were a pain they couldn't discuss. Thea aged — you could see it 'appening. Andy had a good job then, wasn't drinking like he did later, but he . . . well, he resented it. You could see he did. Wouldn't you? Losing your boys just when a father feels he has

255

most to offer them."

"Did feelings ever come out into the open?"

"Never. They come from that class — respectable manufacturing folk — as liked to keep personal things under wraps. Nearest were one year when Mrs P. wanted to take the boys away on holiday. That French valley wi' the castles. The Hoddles had already booked — Portugal or wherever. *That* got around because the boys so wanted to go wi' their aunt. Made no secret of it. And we thought the aunt made it some kind o' trial o' strength."

"Who won?"

"The parents, for once. She were unwise, you see, was Lydia. The parents had t'cards stacked in their favour: they *were* the parents, when all's said and done, and the boys were still under age, and t'holiday had been booked. The boys went wi' their parents — God knows what kind of a time they gave them, but they went wi' them. But it were thought in t'village that Mrs P. lost more than just that round."

"Oh?"

"It were thought — we could ha' got it wrong, o' course — that from that time Maurice went up rather less to his aunt's. Gavin were still dead keen, they were planning his naval career an' all, but we thought as Maurice stayed home more. Could 'a' been just homework, o' course. Maurice were more of a plod-der than Gavin. But we thought that just maybe he'd seen the pain they'd caused their parents. Seen how they'd been sort o' stolen, in an underhand, roundabout sort o' way."

"And Gavin — he never saw?"

"Oh no — Gavin were his aunt's boy, right up to t'time he died. Used to write her great long letters from Washington — postcards to his parents. . . . And Andy loved that lad . . . Andy and Thea both. But Andy wor-shipped the ground he walked on. And if Gavin gave him the time o' day, that were as much as he did give him."

CHAPTER 16

"All I heard was the end of it," Stan Podmore insisted, polishing a glass after Charlie bought his third non-alcoholic wine, something he considered over and above the call of duty. "I was down the other end of the bar and I heard nothing, though of course I could guess what they were talking about."

"How?"

"He'd been boasting how good Mrs Perceval was being to his boys, and everyone in the village knew about her and the Hoddle boys."

"Did you know how Maurice Hoddle felt about her now?"

"No, we didn't. That's why we were interested in him going over to talk to Bellingham."

"What sort of conversation did they seem to be having?"

"Looked to me like young Hoddle was warning Bellingham against his aunt. And like he was pooh-poohing the idea."

"Right," said Charlie. "So then you went close?"

"The till's at that end, see. And I heard

258

Maurice Hoddle say: 'She stole us from our parents, destroyed all our love and respect for them, and killed my brother.'"

"Pretty damning."

Stan Podmore nodded sagely.

"It's what's been said in the village all along. Mind you, I don't think he got through to Nick Bellingham. Once he gets an idea into his head he doesn't give up easily."

"Thick?"

"Two planks."

Outside in the car Charlie made some notes of his conversation with Jim Scattergood and Stan Podmore's overhearings. Then he sat wondering what to do next. A door-to-door enquiry for any sightings or identification of the bearded man was what he was inclined to, but he thought Mike Oddie would think he had wasted the time he had been given on his own. He was just considering his options when a bicycle passed the car, ridden furiously. As it passed him he thought he heard a sob. Looking through the front windscreen he saw Ted Bellingham ride through his front gate, throw his bike down in the drive and run into the house. Charlie gave him a couple of minutes, then got out of the car and strolled leisurely towards the house.

The boy who opened the door to his knock had probably not been crying, or if so only momentarily. Ted was a feeling boy, but not a crying one, Charlie suspected. But he was obviously deeply upset and uncertain.

"Want to talk?" Charlie asked.

"Not really."

"I mean just talk. Chat. Not an interview, nothing taken down, so nothing could be used. I'd have to have your dad here, or a teacher, if I was going to use anything you told me. But you do need someone to talk to, don't you?"

"Well —"

"And you can't talk to your dad or your brother, can you?"

"No."

There was a moment or two more of hesitation, then Ted Bellingham stood aside from the door and let Charlie in, shutting it behind him almost conspiratorially. Then he led the way through to a living room that still showed all the traditional signs of male occupancy without female attention. Ted cleared some dirty clothes off an easy chair for Charlie to sit on, then he himself took one of the dining chairs that was free of encumbrances.

"It was our sports afternoon," he said. "I told the master I wasn't feeling like it, and he understood."

"You're still upset about Mrs Perceval's death, aren't you?"

"Yes." The boy sat thinking. "Yes, in a way. She was good to us. It was interesting going up there. Sort of stimulating. . . ." He suddenly burst out: "I didn't go there because of the money, because she was going to leave us something in her will."

"We never thought you did," said Charlie mildly.

"I bet you did. You noticed Colin's reaction, didn't you?"

"Yes. We're trained to notice things like that."

"He's talking as if that was all he went up for. That he always intended to . . . to worm his way in there, to make her so fond of us that she'd do something like that. I don't like it. That wasn't why I was going up to see her."

"But you did overhear her talking about the will?"

"Yes." He looked down at the floor. "A day or two before she died. We went past the window when she was talking on the phone — I think to her lawyer or something."

"Did you hear when she was going to see him?"

"Yes. Monday."

"And did you talk about it, the two of you, later?"

"No, we didn't. I wished we'd never heard

it. I thought it was . . . sort of nasty. I didn't want to think about it even. But we both of us heard. I don't like Colin saying we were sucking up to her for money!"

Charlie nodded.

"It sounds awful. But are you sure he's not just saying that to justify your seeing so much of her? Some of his mates at school may have been suggesting it was a bit funny for two teenage boys to go calling on a mature lady like Mrs Perceval, and he decided to give that as his reason."

Ted looked at him as if begging to believe him.

"Do you think that's why he's saying it?"

"I don't know. You know your brother better than I do."

Ted's eyes dropped to the floor, but he muttered: "Yes, I expect that's why he's saying it."

"Your parents were quite pleased at your going up there, weren't they?" Charlie asked casually.

"Yes. It meant Dad didn't have to cook for us at night."

"And your mother?"

Ted shook his head, clearly very upset.

"Well, you couldn't say she was pleased. . . . You couldn't even say that she registered. Mum's sick. It's been confirmed she's got

M.E. We go and see her, but mostly she just lies there. Seems like even making conversation is too much effort."

"This must have been upsetting for you both."

"Yes. Specially as Dad didn't understand at all. . . . Lydia thought our dad was a big thickie."

And not only Lydia, Charlie thought.

"Surely she didn't say so?" he said.

"Oh no — she'd never have done that. She was too much of a lady. But somehow you knew — just a second's silence, or a change of subject . . . somehow you knew."

"Did she understand about your mum?"

"When we'd been to the doctor's she did. But I don't think she had much sympathy with illness. I heard her describe a librarian friend of hers as 'a poor creature.' I think she'd decided Mum was 'a poor creature' before she knew that she was ill, and I don't suppose she changed her opinion."

"She seems to have got her opinion across."

"Oh yes, she did. I suppose that's because she always knew what she thought. She'd decided Colin was the brightest of us two, and she didn't hide it."

"Didn't that hurt you?"

Ted thought for a moment.

"No, it's what I've always thought. I did

once or twice mind about Mum — thought she should have been more concerned, should have backed her up, somehow — but I never minded about Colin."

"You minded about your mum, but not your dad?"

"Well, not much. He's not helpless like my mum. And she was quite right: he's not very bright."

"When your dad was in The Wheatsheaf on the night of the murder, you and Colin watched television for a bit, didn't you, and then you went upstairs?"

"Yes."

"Do you have separate bedrooms?"

"Yes, we do. And we went to them. But after about five minutes I remember Colin turned on his transistor." Ted looked straight at Charlie. "Look, I'm not saying Colin went up and murdered her. If you think that I wish I'd never talked to you."

"I don't think that," said Charlie, shaking his head. "I don't think a boy of that age would have had the strength, for a start." This was something Ted had obviously not thought about, but he nodded quickly, relieved. "You're upset because you feel Mrs Perceval was kind to you, and the way Colin is talking makes it sound as if you took advantage of her."

"Yes. And it wasn't like that, not for me. She took an interest, and I appreciated it."

"She deserves better than Colin's reaction. But have you thought maybe she doesn't deserve your reaction either?"

Ted frowned.

"What do you mean?"

"That it's too kind, too favourable to her. It's really a pretty unpleasant business, prising children away from their parents, setting them against them or teaching them to despise them. Whether you understood it or not, that was what was happening. Those silences and changes of subject were calculated by her. She made sure she got her opinions across without stepping over any borderline that would have shown you without question what she was trying to do. But I think you had some unconscious sense of what she was up to. And you knew it had happened in the past with her nephews. I agree she deserved better than to be treated by Colin as a milch cow for a legacy. But I wouldn't give her too much devotion either."

Ted looked at him thoughtfully, then nodded.

"No . . . I suppose what she did for us she did for herself . . . It's funny: when we first talked to her and told her our names, she said 'My fate!' And when we asked her later what she had meant she talked about an ancestor who was prime minister being killed by someone called Bellingham. But we weren't her fate, were we? We had nothing to do with her being killed."

"I'm sure you didn't," said Charlie. Not directly, anyway, he added to himself.

It was barely two when Charlie left the Bellingham semi — a couple of hours or more before Andy Hoddle could be expected home from school. He began the house-to-house enquiry he had contemplated earlier, feeling he could justify giving it two hours of his time. In some houses he was received with suspicion, at others with metaphorical open arms. When they found that the conversation led round to fancy men, via mysterious strangers, most people were anxious to contribute their item of bile about one or other of their neighbours' habits. By the end of the afternoon Charlie had identified four women in the village who were generally thought ("It's well known" was the phrase most people used) to have male friends whom they had reason to want to keep apart from their husbands. In each case the man was known, in three of the four they were men from Bly. None of them had a beard.

Charlie's only stroke of luck — which, like

most luck, sprang from good judgment —
came in the last house he visited. He was just
into a nice piece of character assassination with
Mrs Holmroyd when her daughter Julie came
home from school. It was then that Charlie
decided he could do with that cup of tea Mrs
Holmroyd had offered him earlier on.

"So," he said to Julie when they were alone.
"I've been hearing about you from your boyfriend."

"I don't know about boyfriend," said Julie
Holmroyd, a pretty, rather forward girl.
"Anyway, he won't be for much longer. I'm
looking for someone with a bit more savoir
faire. All he thinks of doing is groping. I hate
gropers."

Charlie thought it was a bit unreasonable
to go into the woods with an adolescent boy
and then complain about being groped. But
he hastened to agree with her.

"The spots are a bad sign," he said. "You
didn't get a better view of the man than Jason
did, I suppose?"

"No — it was just side on. I'd never recognise him again. But I remember a bit more
about the car registration."

"You've talked about it with him?"

"'Course we have. No one talks about anything else. The car was an F registration, like
Jason said, and there was a G and an S in

the number. Something like F four six something, then AGS."

Charlie hastened to put this down in his book.

"That's very helpful. You went down the path past the back of Mrs Perceval's cottage, didn't you?"

"Yes."

"What time would that have been?"

"Don't know. Maybe about twenty to ten . . . I stopped there for a bit."

"Oh? Why was that?"

She looked down, with a sly but not unpleasant grin on her face.

"I thought Colin Bellingham might be there. I think he's dishy."

"But he wasn't there, was he? He'd gone back home."

"Yes. I saw him in their kitchen when I got to the bottom of the path . . . But I think there was someone there."

She shivered. She knew perfectly well who this was likely to be.

"What did you see?"

"I didn't *see* anything, not clearly. The only room that was lit up was the lounge, and there was nobody there. But if you go a bit further down the path you can see the side window of the study. I've often seen Mrs Perceval working there. And when I looked back that night . . . you couldn't see much because there was no light on . . . but somebody *moved* in there. I couldn't see who it was, or whether it was man or woman, but it moved away from the window to where I couldn't see it anymore."

Charlie heard the clink of cups being brought down the hall, and merely whispered: "I hope you find someone with a bit more savoir faire before too long."

After ten more minutes of tea and scandal Charlie escaped to his car and found Mike Oddie there, sitting on the radiator and smoking a rare cigarette in the sun.

"Interesting talk with Oliver Marwick," he said when Charlie came up. "With the cottage the estate will come to between a quarter and a half million — nearer the half, he thinks. She sold well, knew her market, and had no expensive habits. Even her holidays she generally took in connection with the book she was writing, so they were tax-deductible. She felt strongly about income tax, apparently, and thought most of it was spent on people who ought to be standing on their own two feet."

"That's a sum worth killing for."

"Certainly. And the people we're about to visit could reasonably have hoped to inherit."

"If the Hoddles killed her it wasn't for

money," said Charlie, and Mike Oddie nodded agreement.

"They hated her. I wonder if they're going to admit it."

"Oh," said Thea Hoddle when she opened the door to Mike Oddie's knock. "We were half expecting you. Come through . . . I suppose it's about Maurice?"

"Partly about Maurice," said Oddie.

Andy Hoddle was sitting in an armchair in the living room with a pile of exercise books on a coffee-table beside him. There was about him, as there was about Thea, an air of shame-facedness and uncertainty — as if this second visit from the police was something they had expected, but had yet been unable to prepare themselves for.

"We knew we should have mentioned his being here," said Andy, when the policemen were settled down on the sofa.

"Why didn't you?"

Andy and Thea looked at each other.

"It just happened that way . . . It would have complicated things, and it wasn't really relevant."

Oddie decided it was time for plain speaking.

"You mean it would have brought out into the open the real relationship between the two of you, Lydia Perceval, and the boys?"

"Maybe . . . Yes. I suppose you know all about that by now."

"We know something. Let's stick to the facts for the moment. Who was here, how long were they here, why were they here?"

"Maurice and his wife Kelly and their baby were here," said Thea. "They came on Friday, and they were due to leave on Monday. Maurice had an interview lined up in Leeds on Monday. He'd had a tentative offer of a very good job — head of drama with Yorkshire Television. Then on Monday morning he had a phone call asking if he could postpone it till early Tuesday. He squared it with Midlands TV — said the baby had colic — and that's how they came to be here on Monday night."

"I see. Apart from the interview it was purely a family visit, then?"

"Yes. A chance for us to get to know Kelly, whom we've only met two or three times."

"And did you?"

"Get to know her? Yes," said Andy, meditatively. "Interesting girl. Lots of sides to her. Not at all . . . not what Lydia took her to be."

"Oh? And what did Lydia take her to be?"

"In a word, a slut. She'd used four-letter words the only time they'd met. I think she felt condescended to."

271

"I see . . . Well, I suppose a family visit would include a trip up to see Aunt Lydia, wouldn't it?"

"Maurice went," said Thea. "Kelly refused to. He didn't take the baby. Lydia wasn't interested in babies."

"No, she preferred them when they got older, didn't she? Well, I can ask your son himself what happened when he went up there, but can you tell me who was where when Lydia was — possibly — killed? Say around ten on Monday night."

"I was down here with a whisky," said Andy. "Thea was in bed with a book. Maurice went for a drink in The Wheatsheaf. And Kelly was upstairs getting what she calls her beauty sleep — they were due off very early on Tuesday morning."

"I see. All of you unvouched for except Maurice."

"Yes. We made the mistake of not realizing a relation was going to get murdered."

Mike Oddie nodded amiably.

"While your son was in The Wheatsheaf," put in Charlie, "he was heard to say to Nick Bellingham 'She killed my brother.'"

"*Did* he?" said Thea, obviously interested.

"Yes. Was that the view you all took?"

"It sounds a bit melodramatic, doesn't it?" said Thea carefully. "She encouraged Gavin with all sorts of glamorous visions of service life. She was a romantic at heart. She loved seeing him in uniform. Used to say he was Rupert Brooke without the fair hair. We did often feel that Gavin would have gone in for something quite different if it hadn't been for Lydia."

"That all sounds very cool and reasonable," pursued Charlie. "What about a gut reaction? How do you feel *here?*"

Thea's eyes went down to her lap.

"I suppose I feel she killed him," she said.

"Right," said Mike Oddie. "That clears the air, doesn't it? Can we talk about your relationship with your sister?"

Thea was clearly upset, and it was Andy who replied.

"It was very civilised. Thea and Lydia rang each other up periodically. If we were going past the cottage at some time when she wouldn't be working we'd drop in for coffee or a sherry."

"How often would that be?"

"Perhaps once a year . . . There isn't much reason to go up the hill. Sometimes if she was working flat out she'd ask me to get something for her in Halifax. Then I'd normally take it up to her. Until recently I had nothing better to do, and she hated coming to this house."

"Why was that?"

Andy gestured towards the picture of their eldest son in naval finery.

"We thought she hated seeing that. She used to avert her eyes from it. You'll have noticed she had the same picture herself, but she hated us having it."

"But that's absurd!" said Oddie. "Your son . . ."

"In emotional matters Lydia could be absurd," said Thea forcefully. "Like marrying the brother of the man she really loved. She had fought with us for Gavin and she had won. She resented us having any part in him."

"That's how you see it, is it? She won?"

"It's difficult to see it any other way as far as Gavin was concerned," said Andy, sadly. "Oh, we won our small victories. She wanted to pay to send the boys to a public school. Lydia always believed that the inevitable concomitant of a pure heart was a Standard Southern English accent. We put our foot down. On that sort of matter we had some power, just because we were the parents. But Lydia made sure, through having so much to do with them, that there wasn't a trace of Yorkshire in their accents. Maurice likes to use vernacular now and then, being so involved with *Waterloo Terrace,* but he always does it within inverted commas. So in little ways her influence lingers on."

"I gather that at one time Lydia was trying to urge Maurice towards politics," said Charlie.

"Was she? I'm sure you're right. The boys didn't tell us things, you see. . . ."

The husband and wife looked at each other, then quickly away.

"Well," said Oddie, "she certainly failed in that."

"Oh yes," said Andy. "With Maurice she failed almost entirely. That was the danger, wasn't it, of working on adolescent minds. They grow up. Talking about it now it seems pathetic rather than wicked, the fact that Lydia had to have relationships with boys rather than men. She couldn't sustain a relationship of equals. When you come down to it, the relationships after Robert were all with people who were immature."

"*After* Robert?" queried Charlie. "I don't see anything particularly mature about turning your life into a perpetual boy scouts' camp."

CHAPTER 17

Maurice Hoddle walked restlessly up and down the thickly carpeted floor of his office in Midlands Television. The office was a good-sized one, as it needed to be, since it was frequently used for script conferences. It was furnished with the bogus-luxurious anonymity which characterises offices in modern buildings all over the world. Maurice humanised it by untidiness and family snapshots — again, as higher executives of the pleasanter kind did all over the world. Shooting scripts for *Waterloo Terrace* littered both desk and chairs, and a sad pile of unsolicited manuscripts lay by the wall near the door, as if at need it could be used as a door-stop. The baby was in a silver frame on the desk, but massively enlarged on the wall by the door was Kelly, on her first entrance into the Dog and Whistle in *Waterloo Terrace*.

It would have been a restless day for Maurice, even without the imminent arrival of the policemen from Yorkshire. Kelly was auditioning for *William and Annette*, the prestige series Midlands were filming in France in the New Year. She very much wanted the part, but Maurice wasn't at all sure she was right for it. On the other hand, as he freely admitted, Kelly continually surprised him, both in life and in her acting range. What was certainly true was that she would be nervous. He had told the policemen that their coming that day was convenient if they wanted to talk to Kelly as well, since she would be at the studios anyway, but in his heart he wondered if she would behave herself. Quicksilver in her changes of mood at the best of times, the audition would make her behavior totally unpredictable. She could do or say anything, act this or that role in her female repertoire. Surprise, continual stimulation, was one of the things about her that had first attracted him. But one thing was certain: when the subject of Lydia came up Kelly would use the word "cow." She always did.

Maurice went over to the window to calm his nerves. Looking out over Birmingham always calmed his nerves. It was so pre-eminently the city with nothing. Apart from the fact that Kelly was a child of it, and *Waterloo Terrace* a celebration of its people, Maurice would miss nothing about Birmingham. He would be happy — if the job came off — to be back in Yorkshire, particularly a Yorkshire without his aunt Lydia. Lydia had always represented an awkwardness for him, in particular an awkwardness with his parents. He never knew how explicitly he ought to acknowledge the harm she had done, the misery she had caused. Both he and they had shied away from the subject — as English people so often do shy away from discussing the most important things in their lives.

When his secretary showed the policemen in he was relaxed in his welcome. The secretary was instructed to get them all coffee, and while she was setting out cups he studied them both, casting them, as he so often did when he met new people, in soaps. The young black man was easy: he would be a sharp, street-wise hustler in *EastEnders*. If he couldn't act he would be no different from most of the "ethnic" actors in *EastEnders*. But Maurice was pretty sure he would be able to act. Perhaps he was acting now, as a policeman. The older one, Oddie, was harder to cast: a calm, rational, civilised sort of man. Perhaps he would make a suitable husband for one of the older women in *Waterloo Terrace*. Emily Braithwaite, perhaps, who was currently unattached, having gone through three husbands, in the manner of people who stayed a long time in soaps. He pulled himself back to reality as his secretary left the office. This was a serious matter. He must not go off wool-gathering when he needed all his wits about him. He looked at the older man expectantly.

"I can imagine your parents will have spoken to you," Oddie said. "So we can dispense with the preliminaries."

"Yes," said Maurice nodding. "You want to know what I was doing around ten o'clock on the evening Lydia was killed."

"Yes, though we're far from certain that was when she was killed. But can we go back further than that for a start? You went up to see your aunt on Saturday, I believe?"

Maurice grimaced. Oddie noticed a tightening of the muscles over his whole body, and a tension in the hands resting on the arms of his desk chair.

"That's right. It was rather expected of me, though I don't know why: we hadn't got any pleasure from each other's company for a very long time."

"You went on your own?"

"Yes. I thought it would make for less friction. Anyway Kelly would never have come."

"They didn't get on, your aunt and your wife?"

"Chalk and cheese. They'd only met once, but they both took an instant dislike to each other."

"And was there less friction, with you on your own?"

Maurice had already decided on honesty. Quite probably Lydia had told the boys things hadn't gone well.

"No," he said. "Not really, as it turned out. Somehow or other we rubbed each other up the wrong way."

"Any particular reason, sir?"

"No. Everything just seemed to put us on a wrong footing. Her views on my job, memories of Gavin, the boys she was currently taking under her wing. . . . It may be that it all came back to them. That I saw she was starting to do with them what she had done years ago with Gavin and me."

Mike Oddie nodded.

"Perhaps you could say something, then, about how you regarded your aunt — what your relationship was, then and now."

Maurice again grimaced and thought for some seconds. His fingers drummed on the arm-rests, then self-consciously stopped.

"I suppose from her point of view I was damned ungrateful, as well as being unsatisfactory. And if you were compiling a ledger you would have to enter many things on the plus side: she taught us an awful lot, she enlarged our horizons, gave us a great feeling of our *potential* — too great for our talents, perhaps. Going up there was exciting, stretching. Gavin always said she was the person who made you feel you could really do something in the world."

"He was the one most affected by her, wasn't he?"

"Yes."

"And was still devoted to her, up to the time of his death?"

Maurice frowned.

"I suppose so . . . Gavin really enjoyed life, those last few years. He was attached to the Embassy in Washington — young, good-looking, with a glamorous uniform. He was having a whale of a time, and lots of love affairs. But his job was to do with arms sales, so he knew better than most what kind of a war the Falklands thing was going to be. You've seen that photograph of him that Lydia and my parents have, have you?"

"Yes."

"In point of fact I gave Mum and Dad that copy, said he'd meant it for them. . . . But when he sent it, just after the Argentine troops invaded, he wrote: 'I look at this chap and wonder whether it is me at all.'"

"What do you think he meant by that?"

"That somehow he'd . . . taken a wrong turning. Got into something that wasn't really what he wanted to do at all, and wasn't right for."

"Aren't you reading a lot into it?"

"Yes . . . I hate to think of Gavin being Lydia's boy right up to the end."

"Did he know he was going to be involved in the war himself?"

"I think he had a shrewd idea. A day or two later he was called back to London, told he was going to be involved in PR and liaison with the press. He phoned me a few days before he sailed. I remember him saying: 'I don't see *me* in this war. I just can't see what it has to do with me.' That's why I've always believed that he did get some feeling, before he died, that Lydia's influence had set him on the wrong path."

"Did you say the subject of your brother was one of the things that you and your aunt argued about last Saturday?"

"He came up. I was foolish to let it. Lydia felt she had some kind of exclusive rights in Gavin."

"You began to have doubts about your aunt, didn't you, a long time before your brother did — if he ever did have them?"

"Yes, I did. I don't remember when it was, but I know I was still at school."

"Someone in the village suggested it was when you went on holiday with your parents to Portugal," Charlie put in.

Maurice turned to him.

"Do you know, I think that could be right.

How closely the whole thing must have been observed! . . . God, that holiday! We resented going, because we'd wanted to go with Lydia to see the Loire Valley castles. Looking back, I think Lydia dangled that prospect before us *after* she knew that Dad had booked for us all to go to Cascais. It was a deliberate trial of strength. And if she lost that one, I don't suppose it felt much like that to Mother and Father. We behaved disgustingly. We wouldn't swim, we said the food was 'provincial' . . . God, we were little shits! But then we were pretty horrible to them much of the time — ignored them, put their opinions, their hopes for us in second place, or nowhere at all. . . . And then suddenly — and it could have been on that holiday, because I remember being much happier in the second week — something hit me like a thunderbolt: 'These are our parents,' I remember thinking. 'It's our mother and father that we're doing this to.' I don't know how or why it happened. . . ."

"It's called growing up," said Oddie.

"Right. I suppose that was it." Maurice paused and meditated, putting the course of his own life in order in his mind. "Anyway, that was the beginning of the end of Lydia's influence over me."

"Was it about then that she gave up the

idea of grooming you for politics?" Charlie asked.

"That was rather earlier, as I remember," said Maurice, his forehead creased. "By the time I . . . grew out of her she had had a series of vague ambitions for me, but they were nothing more than that: she was really taken up with Gavin. She was a one-man woman. But the politics thing illustrates something about Lydia: her plans and hopes bore very little relation to the person she made them for. Gavin could be moulded into the form of a dashing naval hero — though I always felt it was essentially a front, because in spite of his enjoying the Washington social life Gavin was really a loner. And you're never alone on a ship, are you? But Gavin passed muster, as I say. I was never going to pass muster as a politician. It wasn't me at all. I didn't enjoy speaking in public, I had no political convictions one way or the other, and still haven't, I simply wasn't outgoing enough. At best I'd have been an uneasy, Edward-Heath-like figure. But Lydia decided the nation needed saving, so I was to be the nation's saviour. They were essentially plans for herself — for herself through me. It was ridiculous."

"Do you think Mrs Perceval had relationships with adolescents rather than men because she wanted to mould them?"

"Yes. I can say that now, of course. I couldn't see it at the time."

"She liked playing God?"

"Yes. Even with the marriage to Jamie: people say it came about because she couldn't get Robert, and I'm sure that's true, but the other thing was she thought she could mould him. The give and take of really adult relationships wasn't in her: she had to give, make, others had to take, be made. And she found she couldn't mould Jamie. I remember her saying once: 'He was like jelly in my hands.' That's the only time I remember her talking about her marriage."

"Do you think she continued to love Robert?" Charlie asked.

Maurice nodded his head.

"In her way. I'm not sure 'love' is the word I'd use. She talked about him a lot, played up what he was doing — because a lot of the treks and endurance feats he went in for didn't amount to a great deal. She always made sure he had a letter with all the family news when he came through or came out. I don't suppose he gave a monkey's fart for family news. He hardly ever came up North, hardly ever visited his parents, I believe. Yes, in a way he was still a hero to Lydia. But she loved Gavin."

Oddie decided it was time to bring him back to the present.

"You say your visit on Saturday wasn't a happy one, sir."

Maurice was glad he had decided on honesty on that point. If Lydia hadn't said anything about it to the boys, she was pretty sure to have said something to that cleaning lady of hers. He nodded vigorously.

"Not particularly happy. Let's say it was tense. You have to remember she ruined my relationship with my parents, and that it's never quite been repaired. There always is this awkwardness between us, the shadow of my . . . treachery. Actually, having Kelly and Matthew with me made things easier."

"Lightened the atmosphere?"

"More a case of them being a part of my life that has no connection or association with Lydia. Anyway, being with my parents, seeing them afresh as such likeable people, so innocent of wishing harm, meant that I wasn't disposed to be easy on Aunt Lydia. Meeting her in London or Birmingham was usually less tense."

"Did your wife's view of her add to your feeling that you needn't be easy on her?"

"Maybe. Kelly's very alive to pretensions and small snobberies — of the sort that Lydia mistook for standards."

"Perhaps you could tell us what you actually did on the evening of the murder, sir," said Oddie.

There was a perceptible relaxation in Maurice.

"Oh, that's easy. Of course I've thought about it. We were all together, talking and watching television till something after nine. Then Kelly decided to turn in early — we were to be up at six and away by seven thirty the next morning, and she gets tired with the baby. Mum was getting ready for bed, but I thought I'd go and have a drink in The Wheatsheaf, see if any old friends from the village were there."

"Did you ask your father to go with you?"

"Yes, but he preferred a whisky at home, because he had some teaching to look over."

"And did you find any of your old friends in The Wheatsheaf?"

"Nobody of my own age — no old school-friends. Most of them would have left the village, I suppose. But I knew practically everyone there. The Wheatsheaf is where I had my first pint of bitter— with my dad, who was wishing he was having it with Gavin." He smiled a lopsided smile. "Life has been a bastard to him. Anyway, I was chatting away to Syd Horrocks, who used to be the village butcher, and he was making lubricious allusions to my wife — because Kelly's visit has been a minor sensation in the village — no, a major one: they'll be talking about it till the turn of the century. Anyway, after we'd been talking a bit I realised there was this berk down the other end of the bar talking about Lydia."

"What *time* was this?" Charlie asked.

"Well, say I went to The Wheatsheaf around half past nine —"

"You didn't meet Mrs Perceval and the boys on the way there?"

"No, I didn't. Of course I'd have stopped for a chat if I had. Well, I suppose I became conscious of this Mr — I've forgotten his name."

"Bellingham."

"Right. I became conscious of him say towards ten. After a second or two I remembered who he was."

"You'd met him?"

"Not exactly met. He'd lurched over to our table when we were in the Maple Tree the previous Friday. He didn't remember me, but I remembered him. And of course I listened pretty intently as soon as I did, because the boys had come in while I was at Lydia's, and it was — well, quite an experience."

"Yourself when young?" Oddie suggested.

"Exactly — like an old film re-run. Just

the situation with me and Gavin in the seventies. Only this time, I gathered, it was the younger one who was the favourite."

"Yes — and he seems the one who was most out for what he could get," said Charlie.

"Really? But then Lydia was never very good at fathoming people — not people in the flesh. She never understood Gavin — as I tried to explain to her last weekend, to her great offence. Anyway, eventually I went over to this — Bellingham did you say? — and tried to warn him that small doses of Lydia might be good for his boys, but that quite soon she would try to prise them away from their parents, especially as I gathered that his wife was sick and likely to be so for a long while."

"We hear you didn't get through to him."

"Ah — you've talked to people about it, have you? No — not one millimetre into his thick skull. Room for one idea in his head and that's all. Eventually I got angry, went back to the other end of the bar, finished my beer and left."

"What time did you leave, sir?" Oddie asked.

"Oh, about twenty past ten. I was back in time for the end of the ITV ten o'clock news — they had a 'funny' on as usual: you know, talking goldfish, that kind of thing."

"And was your father still up?"

"Oh yes. We had a bit of a chat, quite cosy together, and we both went up to bed about eleven."

"And did you meet anyone in the street on the way home, sir?" Charlie asked.

"Nobody that I remember. Nobody at all, I think. One or two cars went by. . . ."

"You don't remember the makes of any of them?" Charlie asked.

Maurice laughed at him.

"Give me a break! Remember the makes of cars that pass you in the night? Of course I d—"

"Arrest my 'usband, Inspector, for 'e is ze guilty man," said a voice from the door, in execrable *'Allo 'Allo* French English. Charlie turned and his stomach churned over, along with other physical effects that made him glad he was sitting in a chair with a notebook on his lap. No wonder the advent of Kelly Marsh had been a milestone in the social life of Bly!

"My wife, Kelly Marsh," said Maurice, getting up and going over to her. "She's here auditioning for *William and Annette,* our next year's prestige mini-series."

"Ah, that would be William Wordsworth and the French Revolution, wouldn't it?" Oddie said, shaking the hand that Kelly had free of her baby. "'Bliss was it in that dawn to be alive'?"

"Yes. Wordsworth omitted to mention that by mid-morning you were *lucky* to be alive," said Maurice. "God, don't I sound like Lydia? She was never a friend to revolutions. Yes, Kelly's auditioning for the part of Annette."

"I thought eet would be good to breeng my bébé," said Kelly, smiling guilelessly up at the policeman. "Ze innocent fruit of our illeeecit passion. . . . Who *was* this prat Wordsworth anyway?"

She was wearing a modest, calf-length woollen dress with lace around the neck, an outfit far from her usual style. However she bundled the baby into Maurice's arms and perched herself on his desk, raising her skirts to above her knees and aiming them directly at Charlie. His face may have remained impassive but his heart started doing the one hundred metres. He noticed that Maurice was looking at his wife with an expression that could only be described as excited.

"Don't take any notice of Kelly," he said happily. "She knows perfectly well who Wordsworth was. She's got Ordinary Level English —"

"Graham Greene and Chinua Achebe was what we did."

"— she's even got an A level —"

"Domestic bloody Science, if you'll believe it."

"— but she'd die rather than tell anybody because she's such a frightful inverted snob."

"Being a slut suits me," explained Kelly to Charlie. "Because it's closest to what I really am."

"Did you play the slut or the A level student when you met Lydia Perceval?" Charlie asked.

"The slut, of course," said Kelly with relish, laughing aloud and hitching her skirt an inch or two further up her thigh. "You don't think Old Mother Starch-in-her-Drawers would be impressed by an A level in Domestic Science, do you?"

"Did you meet in Bly?"

Kelly Marsh smiled, and licked her lips in reminiscence.

"No. Last weekend was my first visit. She came down to Birmingham to do a chat spot on a daytime programme. BBC, of course. Even that was rather beneath her, so she tried to convey, and we felt that she really came down to confirm that Maurice's choice of wife showed he'd gone irretrievably to the bad."

"Which you proceeded to demonstrate," said Maurice amiably.

"Well, the moment the old cow saw me she

drew herself up, like a Victorian bishop's wife who's found out her son's married a fallen woman. Anyone would add a few 'fuckings' to the conversation, faced with that."

"And Lydia became glacial," Maurice remembered. "She had no social devices she could use against that sort of thing. If it had been a child she would have known what to do, but against an adult she was powerless. She just clammed up. She was supposed to go out with us for a meal that night, but she rang later and said she was too tired."

"Luckily I'd got something in for us," said Kelly wickedly.

"And was that the only contact you had with her before last weekend?" Oddie asked.

"It was the only contact I had with her full stop," said Kelly emphatically. "You don't think I'd go up there to let Lady Sneer look down her long bony nose at me again, do you?" She smiled, with a hint of relish in her smile. "Mind you, I'd have quite liked meeting her in the street, so I could give her the full treatment again in the hearing of the locals. And the locals would have enjoyed it too. But I wasn't going to climb Mount Olympus to let her condescend to me in her own house. Maurice went on his own."

"And at the time she was murdered you were in bed, we understand," Oddie said.

"In bed alone, sleeping prettily like the heroine of a Barbara Cartland."

"With nobody to vouch for you, unfortunately."

"Only young Piss-my-nappy here," she said, ruffling the sparse hair on Matthew's head, as he lay in his father's arms. "He was in a cot by our bed."

"Much too young to testify, I'm afraid," said Oddie, smiling.

"He'd have testified to my absence if he'd woken and cried — which he does all the time — and I hadn't been there to take him up," Kelly pointed out. "No, I don't think I'd risk it, just to kill the woman who had a terrible influence on my husband fifteen or twenty years ago. That's a *terrible* motive, by the way: you wouldn't get away with that even on *Murder, She Wrote*. Or have you dreamed up something better?"

Mike Oddie had to admit that he hadn't, and got up to leave.

"I hope the audition went well," he said politely.

"Pretty well, I think." She jumped off the desk and clasped her hands together. "I sink I play ze pretty French bourgeoise vairy preetily. Poor leetle muzzer of William's child, abandonated by ze oh-so-respectable English poet." She put off the accent with a wave of

294

cessing up the endless aisle of some limitlessly extended cathedral.

"At this rate we're going to keep the next corpse waiting," whispered Andy beside her.

Charlie Peace was talking vigorously in the police canteen in Halifax when Mike Oddie touched his hand and jerked his head towards a table near the window.

"See that WPC over there?"

"WPC Bilton. What about her?"

"Her nickname for you is 'Heavenly Peace'."

Charlie felt stopped in his tracks.

"Well?"

"You inspire that sort of devotion in the uniformed breast of a WPC, and all you can do is sit there rabbitting on about men with beards."

Charlie regarded him thoughtfully.

"I suppose it is better than 'The Peace that Passeth Understanding,' which is what one of the inspectors at the Yard used to call me. . . . You don't go much on the man with the beard, do you?"

"Oh, I go on him. I'd like to know who he was, what he was doing there. But I'm not going to place him so much in the front of the picture that I lose sight of Maurice Hoddle or Colin Bellingham, or any of the others."

the hand. "At any rate I think I'll be through to the next stage, which is the best three or four. And if I get it — goodbye to Sharon the barmaid forever."

But Charlie thought there was always going to be a bit of Sharon the barmaid about Kelly Marsh.

CHAPTER 18

Lydia's funeral was a compromise, of the kind she herself had despised in life. Thea had ruled out a church funeral, knowing that Lydia had had no faith since her late teens. She had arranged to have the — not *service*, but what did you call it? — ceremony at a crematorium near Halifax. When Lydia's editor at Magister Books rang to offer condolences and enquire about the state of her final manuscript Thea conscripted him to come up and give an address by assuring him, with Robert's agreement, that he could take the manuscript away with him. Knowing Lydia had had no taste in music, and having little herself, she contacted Lydia's library friend at Boston Spa and asked her to suggest something, because she felt a funeral without music would seem odd. But the question of who was to lead the ceremony was the real problem. She didn't even consider herself or Andy, since their feelings about Lydia were so generally known. Robert was the obvious candidate, but he decisively negatived the proposal. It was as much as he would do to get along to the service, he said: funerals gave him the creeps. In the end Thea

accepted the undertakers' suggestion of using the tame cleric on the books of the crematorium to officiate, so Lydia went to her rest blessed by non-denominational prayers and with bland promises of some kind of after-life that she would have scorned.

Looking around the crematorium's chapel Thea wished she had gone the whole hog and had a church service. It would at least have had a dignity appropriate to Lydia in life. And perhaps if she had arranged something in the little church at Bly more of the village would have come. As it was the chapel was sparsely filled, and the impression of an occasion unworthy of Lydia was reinforced by the chapel itself: a gimcrack affair built in the sixties with cheap wood and half-hearted suggestions of gothic about the windows.

The music was very grand, though. The "Gloria" from Cherubini's Coronation Mass for Charles X. Grave, stately, unshowy music, with moments of radiant joy. Dorothy Eccles had been very good and had procured the record herself. Wasn't it rather long, though? Thea saw the all-purpose clergyman sneak a look at his watch, and the man from Magister Books shuffle his notes. On and on the music went, unwinding in graceful lines, speaking the unhurried certainties of another age, so that one saw the king and his attendants pr

Charlie Peace made a dismissive gesture.

"Colin Bellingham could never have done it. A boy of thirteen wouldn't have the strength."

"What about if both the boys were in it, and one of them held her? . . . All right, I don't seriously think that's what happened, but I'm not ruling it out and neither should you. You're in danger of getting tunnel vision."

"All right. Point taken. Totally open mind . . . but one last thing before we leave him."

Oddie groaned.

"Go on."

"We have a bearded man on the scene whom nobody in the village knows anything about. Now, you can be damned sure with that village that this means his business was up the hill, because if it had been down someone or other would have known. So we have a bearded man on the scene at about the time that Lydia Perceval was killed. That's all I'm saying."

"And it's something I'm not denying. Let's go up and see if anything's come through from the Anchorage police. That way we can at least rule out Robert Loxton. Smile at WPC Bilton as you go by. Smile beatifically."

"Beatifically's not in me. And Kelly Marsh has spoiled me for WPCs. Why didn't I transfer to Birmingham?"

★ ★ ★

The noble choral music drew with agonising slowness to an end. A tear fell down Dorothy Eccles's cheek. Such splendour, such vision! She had been right to choose it. It provided a fitting tribute to Lydia. If she had had an ear for music, this was the sort of sound she would have appreciated. *Noble* music.

When the clergyman, suppressing a sigh of relief, rose to speak Dorothy Eccles looked at him critically. A very nondescript little man. Not somebody Lydia would have given a second glance at.

"We are here to pay a last tribute to a writer whose work has given pleasure to millions."

Dorothy Eccles sniffed. He could have been talking about Barbara Cartland! The point about Lydia's books was not that they gave pleasure but that they were works of scholarship. They enlarged our understanding of people and events.

She shot a quick glance to her right. That must be the nephew who had disappointed Lydia so grievously. No sign of his wife, whom Lydia said was so appalling. Altogether not many people here at all. . . .

She shifted her head a little to the left and then a little to the right, trying not to give the impression that she was counting. Really a very meagre attendance for someone of

Lydia's distinction. No doubt the sister was to blame. She had never appreciated what Lydia had done for her and her boys. She was much to blame: as sister she should have made more effort to see that a respectable number paid tribute to Lydia in death.

It did not occur to her to wonder why effort should have been necessary.

"Herself the descendent of one of this country's prime ministers — and, sadly, one who was also tragically slain in his prime. . . ."

Thea Hoddle looked down into her lap and grinned. She had given the vaguely reverend gentleman this tidbit when she had spoken to him about the service, but she had always had her doubts about Lydia's claim. She had come up with it in her late teens, when she was more romantic and ancestral than historically meticulous. She thought it was more in the nature of a guess or a hope than a fact. It was, when she came to think about it, the central fact about Lydia that the clear gaze she cast on other people's characters and lives faltered when she came to her own. She imposed an order on her life, but only through fabricating legends. She was, like most people, thoroughly self-deceived. Had one of her self-deceptions led to her death?

★ ★ ★

When Mike and Charlie got to their temporary office in the Halifax police headquarters they found a report from Anchorage — a lengthy piece that showed that their contact there had done his job properly. Robert Loxton had been at Karen Paulson's flat from Friday night until late on Monday evening, when he had flown to Washington. Occasionally he had gone to collect messages from the Hilton; he had prepared for and given his press conference on Monday morning; otherwise he had been satisfying those needs which are not catered for in U.S. Army Emergency Rations. His presence in the flat was vouched for by several residents of the flat complex where Karen Paulson lived, and by the proprietors of a newsagent's and a liquor store in its vicinity, where he had bought newspapers and wine.

"Makes Anchorage sound a bit like Bly," said Charlie. "Watched by a thousand eyes."

The policeman who had done the investigation and the report had also faxed them the account in the *Anchorage Observer* of the news conference. It was a page-long piece with picture, and the inspector had marked the place where the date and time were mentioned. Oddie stared closely at the picture.

"That's him all right," he said, getting his

eyes close to the bearded figure sitting alone at a long table on a platform. "Quite definitely him. If you had any idea it might be his mate standing in for him you can give it up. Robert Loxton is out — no question of that. . . . Well, I'm just nipping out for some cigarettes and chocolate, then I've got to prepare a report for the Chief Super —"

But he closed the door without a response from Charlie. Something had clicked in his mind — or rather, it was more physical than that: something in his stomach had turned over. Odd that something so physical should be the consequence of a revelation. He sat by the desk, staring at the fax sheets from Alaska.

Robert Loxton sat in the cheap and nasty little chapel hating every moment of it. This was the last funeral he was ever going to go to. Probably the last anyone would expect him to go to: apart from Jamie he had no close family and no close ties. That was how he liked it.

Lydia's editor was talking bilge about the beauty of her manuscripts, and how he never needed to change anything, "even had I dared." Actually he remembered Lydia holding forth one evening in a restaurant about the decline in editing, and how manuscripts were sent straight to the printers with all their manifest errors and absurdities uncorrected. Like almost everything else in the modern world, according to Lydia, editing had sadly declined.

"Passionately committed to truth, eager against error. . . ."

What crap! Lydia had her illusions like the rest of us, and they had blinded her to truth. . . . But passionate — yes, once. The word suddenly released another memory of Lydia. She was with him in bed — it must have been in the Pimlico flat, some time in the late fifties — and he had just told her that for him marriage was simply not on the agenda. Her face had creased with fury, and she had turned to him and battered her fists repeatedly on his bare chest. Then she had lain back exhausted on the pillow, and after a time had said: "I expect you're right."

Funny how things had worked out.

When Mike returned with the cigarettes and chocolate he found his constable with a smile of pure triumph on his face. He didn't remember ever seeing Charlie in that state, irony and merry cynicism being much more his line.

"We forgot," said Charlie, turning to him, "the other man with the beard in this case."

"The other? God protect me! A third?"

"First Jamie Loxton, who has something

close to an alibi if Lydia was killed at ten. Second Robert Loxton, who has a perfectly wonderful alibi whenever she was killed. . . ."

"And?" said Mike Oddie, frowning.

"And Walter Denning."

"Who? Never heard of him."

"Walter Denning, the man who spent four months on Mount McKinley with Robert Loxton."

"But why? —"

"Remember when he talked to us about the press conference in Anchorage? He said 'We had a press conference starting at ten.' But look at that picture. Where's his partner? You'd expect him to be there, wouldn't you? But he isn't. You can see the whole table Loxton sat behind. He was on his own."

"Does the report say anything about him?"

"He's named at the start of the report. Later someone asked what kind of person went in for these endurance feats — interesting question! — and Robert Loxton said: 'Loners, and people interested in the human body and what it can take.' Then someone commented that for a loner he gave a pretty good press conference, and he replied that it was a skill he'd learnt over the years. 'My partner doesn't like this sort of thing at all,' he said."

"'My partner.' Sounds as if they'd done

several of these expeditions together."

"That's what I thought."

"Still, you haven't got a motive worth a bean."

Charlie spread out his hands eloquently.

"They sit there, bivouacked in the snow and ice, and they talk about what they're going to do next, how they're going to raise the money for it. Robert Loxton is getting older, he's been at this sort of thing quite a while. Even when Maurice Hoddle was growing up he said that some of Loxton's expeditions didn't amount to a great deal. The present one didn't. And they sit there, these two schoolboys who somehow never grew up, and they plan one last, grand expedition. And Robert Loxton says: 'I'm my cousin Lydia's heir. If only she would die. . . .' "

"It's very flimsy and totally conjectural."

"And when they come back to Anchorage and book into the hotel they're nominally staying at, they find among the mail Lydia's letter with all the family news. And among the news she says casually: 'There are two boys from the village that I've got interested in. . . .' And they both wonder how long Robert will remain her heir."

The editor was still droning on, having conspicuously failed to edit his own speech.

Ted Bellingham thought: my first funeral. I'd have expected it would have been Grandma Bellingham or one of the uncles or aunts — someone I didn't care much about. But I did care about Lydia Perceval. Whatever her faults, whatever she would have done if she'd lived, I did care about her. Things are never going to be the same again, not quite the same. In a way I've grown up. . . . And things between me and Colin are never going to be the same.

Colin Bellingham thought: that must be the cousin who gets the loot. Lucky bugger! Look at that phoney eyes-fixed-on-a-distant-prospect look. I wonder if he's homosexual. A lot of these explorers and loners are. Perhaps it might be worth while going up to talk to him afterwards. . . .

"Above all," said the editor, who seemed to be responding to some sign from the undertakers at the back of the chapel, "Lydia was a perfectionist. Her life, like her books, had clarity and shape. It is that shape which was so hideously destroyed by the person who killed her."

Is he here today? all but one of the congregation wondered.

"What have you done so far?" asked Mike Oddie, after considering for some moments.

307

"I rang a friend in a travel office in Leeds," said Charlie. "She said anyone flying from Anchorage to Britain would almost certainly come via Seattle. She gave me the names of the airlines who ran direct or near-direct flights from Seattle to Britain that weekend. I figured that he might use a false name on an internal U.S. flight, but unless he had a false passport already prepared he'd use his own name on the intercontinental one."

"You've contacted the airlines?"

"Yes, I'm just waiting for them to ring back. They were all very helpful. Apparently with computers it's a relatively straightforward thing to check."

Oddie shook his head.

"Of course, it doesn't prove anything, even if he did fly back that weekend."

"It would be interesting though, wouldn't it? You'd expect him to enjoy a few days resting, a bit of hotel luxury, maybe have a girl lined up like Robert Loxton."

"Maybe. On the other hand maybe the two couldn't stand each other by the end of the four months, and all this Walter Denning wanted was to put a distance between himself and Robert Loxton. Or maybe these endurance freaks don't think like the rest of us — that would figure . . . I wonder if these two really were regular partners. What had they done together before?"

"Who would know?" Charlie pondered. "Robert Loxton is a Yorkshireman. The *Yorkshire Post* may have monitored his activities more closely than a national paper would."

"I hope you'd have phrased that differently if you'd been talking to one of their reporters," said Oddie, slipping over to the office's second desk. "They think they *are* a national newspaper. I'll ring Frank Wiggins. He's a good friend, and he'll get any info he doesn't have to hand. I'll use this phone so as to leave that one free for your airline."

And in fact while he was talking to Frank Wiggins at the *Yorkshire Post* Charlie's phone rang, and he saw the young man taking down details with a smile of intense satisfaction on his face.

When Thea had asked Dorothy Eccles to organise the music she had stressed that Lydia had not been a Christian. This had put Dorothy in a quandary, because she felt that the congregation (she had imagined something very much larger than had actually assembled) should have something to *sing*. How else could one pay tribute to the dead one? And when it came down to it there wasn't much else a mass of people could sing except hymns.

After all, they did that even at the Cup Final.

In the end she compromised and chose "Jerusalem." She reasoned that it was Blake, that the words were wonderfully evocative, and nobody was quite sure what they meant, except that they didn't mean what the Women's Institutes thought they meant.

And so it was with Blake and Parry that the funeral service ended. Molly Kegan had borne up through everything else, had even felt spasms of irritation at the fatuities of the clergyman and the prosiness of the editor. But music got to her, as music so often does. The straggly vocalism of the congregation singing of bows of burning gold brought tears to her eyes, then racking sobs that forced her to sit down and hide her face in her hands.

Thea wondered to see it. Her sister was genuinely mourned.

"Stop looking like a cat who's knocked over the cream jug," said Oddie as he put the phone down. "Give me the details."

"He travelled by Continental, leaving Seattle Saturday at one P.M. and arriving at Heathrow on Sunday morning at seven twenty."

"Right. We have our man back in Britain in plenty of time for the murder. Frank Wiggins is pretty sure Walter Denning is a regular

310

partner of Loxton's. He remembers an expedition to Antarctica to monitor ecological damage. He says it was sponsored by the Royal Geographical Society."

"Could you ring them?"

"I'm just wondering what would be the right approach."

They both pondered.

"They'll know about Lydia's murder, and they'll know Robert Loxton's connection with her," Charlie said slowly. "It's been in all the papers. Couldn't you just say you're checking his alibi?"

"Not a bad idea. Get me the number, will you?"

A minute later Mike was talking to the Secretary of the Society.

"This is the West Yorkshire Police. I'm investigating the murder of Lydia Perceval, the writer."

"Oh really?" said a cool, genteel voice. "Awful business. Hers was one of the better books on T. E. Lawrence."

"I'm sure it was. Now, purely as a formality I'm having to check the alibi of Robert Loxton, who's the heir. He was in Alaska at the time."

"I believe so. Not one of our expeditions."

"No, but he was with a man called Walter Denning, who'd been with him on one of your

311

expeditions in the past."

"The Antarctic one. Nineteen eighty-four. Yes, I remember him. He was in and out of here quite a bit during the preparations for the survey. Man of few words, but very capable."

"Do you have an address for him?"

Oddie wondered whether the man would ask why he couldn't get it from Robert Loxton, but he didn't.

"I must have him on my files here somewhere. . . . Oh yes. He's got a flat in Kensington. 23 Museum Gardens, SW3."

"Thank you. You're most kind. Pure formality, of course."

"Loxton will be well set up, we hear?"

"There is a fairly considerable estate."

"Maybe he'll be able to do that Gobi Desert trip he's been trying to get finance for for years."

"Maybe he will."

As he rang off he saw that Charlie was already on his phone. Charlie had been in the uniformed branch at Scotland Yard for two years, and there was nothing you could teach him about checking people and their cars.

"Yes, Walter Denning, of 23 Museum Gardens, London SW3. . . . Fiesta, registration number F462 EGS. Thank you. Thank you very much indeed."

312

CHAPTER 19

It was not until three weeks later, when both of them had gone on to other and less interesting cases, that Mike Oddie and Charlie Peace were able to get together over a drink and really talk about the people in the case. They got two pints and two doorstep beef sandwiches at the Flying Fox, a seedy pub ten minutes from the West Yorkshire Police Headquarters in Leeds, Charlie wondering under his breath to Mike why barmaids in real pubs were frowsty and dim, and totally unlike the barmaids in soaps. They took their drinks over to a table in a lonely corner of the saloon bar and settled down for a good natter.

"The forensic case against Denning is watertight," said Oddie. "I doubt we could have got him on the young people's evidence, because their identification of the car could have been pulled to pieces in court. But with forensic matching the strands of rope on his gloves to those in Lydia Perceval's throat — not to mention the earth in the tread of his car tyres — then there isn't much defending counsel can argue, in my opinion."

"No . . . Funny about cases based on forensic evidence," said Charlie, stretching his long legs out under the table.

"They don't somehow satisfy, do they? Why is that, do you think?"

"Because Forensic always behave as if they are infallible, and their evidence unquestionable?" suggested Mike. "As if the dingo baby case had never happened, not to mention the Birmingham Six."

"Maybe . . . and maybe because the forensic case always leaves so many questions unanswered, I think."

"It ignores the human side?"

"Right. That's exactly it. Means you don't even have to ask questions like why on earth Denning kept his gloves."

Mike supped deep in his beer.

"Arrogance?"

"Either that or a subconscious wish to be caught."

"I didn't see any sign of that. I never met a suspect who stood up for his rights better. That stubborn refusal to answer my questions without a solicitor present — a lot of people try it, but I've never seen it done so successfully."

"Didn't you feel he was in a way impressive?"

"Yes, I did. More so than Loxton."

"They're different types, aren't they?" suggested Charlie, setting down his glass. "In Loxton there's always this trace of Enid Blyton: *Two Go Adventuring Again*."

"Right. He's an adventurer, while Denning is — what should we call him? — an explorer, perhaps."

"That classic look with the eyes fixed on some distant object nobody else can see. Loxton tries it, but he has it. Makes the partnership between them difficult to understand."

"Oh, I don't think so," said Oddie. "They had more than enough in common to make it quite understandable. If you want to put it in old-fashioned terms (terms my wife would strongly object to) you could say that Denning was the male side of the partnership, Loxton the female. I don't mean that sexually, of course."

"Of course not. Denning the doer, Loxton the player, Denning the adult, Loxton the child. That makes it understandable that it should be Denning who goes off and does the murder, even though he's not the one who directly benefits."

"It was the essence of the plan that the murderer *had* to be the one who didn't benefit at all."

"True . . . Do you think we have a case

against Robert Loxton that will stick?"

"Don't you?"

"I suppose so," said Charlie, but with a dubious expression on his face. "The two of them thinking up the plan while they were out there on the frozen wastes, and putting it into execution as soon as they got back to civilisation — that's a nice, neat case that will appeal to a jury."

"That was your idea in the first place. And there's nothing wrong with a nice, neat case that will appeal to a jury. What worries you about it?"

"Just the fact that there is an equally good alternative scenario."

"Which is?"

Charlie Peace spread out his hands.

"Pretty much Robert Loxton's account of things. That they sat in their bivouac planning to murder Lydia in jest. The theatrical 'perfect murder' which never is. People do that, you know: schoolkids plan to kill a teacher they hate; nurses think up ways to murder matron."

"Husbands plan to kill wives, and wives husbands. Oh, I know. I've done it myself in my time."

"But just as a joke, an exercise . . . a feat of mental gymnastics. And that's how Robert Loxton saw it: a piece of 'if only we could' that would ensure one big, last feat of exploration and endurance. So when they got back to Anchorage they're relaxing in the Hilton Hotel and Robert reads out Lydia's letter, which was waiting for them."

"That was a brilliant guess on your part."

"Compliment accepted. What Lydia actually said was: 'There are two boys in the village, boys whose mother seems to be sick, whom I'm seeing a lot of, so it's quite like old times. They remind me so much of Gavin and poor Maurice.'"

"Wasn't that an interesting formulation?" Oddie said. "Gavin died a hero, so it's Maurice, who didn't live up to her plans for him, who is 'poor' — a poor fish, in her eyes."

"Right. So he reads out the letter, and they laugh, and Robert says 'Better get the job done quickly before she changes her will.' And then he goes off to his Karen and it's only after he's gone back to the hotel two or three times that he realizes Denning is no longer there, and then he starts to wonder. . . .'"

"Doesn't that scenario raise all sorts of questions about the character of Walter Denning?" asked Oddie. "He strings along with Loxton's joke all the time they are out there on Mount McKinley, then acts on it for real as soon as they get back to base."

"I think every scenario we've considered

raises questions about the character of Walter Denning," said Charlie.

"Fair enough. Let's have another pint. My current case of a compulsive shoplifter is not nearly as fascinating as the murder of Lydia Perceval."

When he got back to the table with two fresh pints Oddie said:

"Don't you think the truth probably lies somewhere between the two — as the truth so often, messily and unsatisfactorily, does? That they did talk about Lydia's murder together, always as a joke, but that Robert knew his companion, knew his compulsive wish to get this Gobi Desert expedition off the ground, and always half hoped that he'd take it seriously and go off and do it?"

"That would make us feel better about a jail sentence for him," agreed Charlie. "But there again: a jail sentence for 'half hoping' something?"

"He may well get off," Oddie pointed out. "He'll certainly have a good counsel. Denning may say something to back his story up."

"Denning saying *anything* of substance would be a red-letter day," grumbled Charlie. "After all the hours and hours of questioning them and sitting in on your questioning them I feel I *know* Loxton. I don't feel I know Denning at all."

"That's often the case with these explorers — compulsive loners who in a sense want to hide themselves. Often they turn out to be very odd people — Burton was, Stanley was. Odd, and rather unpleasant. But to their contemporaries they seemed to be unfathomable mysteries."

"Why did he *strangle* her?" asked Charlie.

"It's rather a neat method of murder," said Oddie. "No bullet for the ballistics people, no messy blood."

"But so chancy."

"Not so very, for someone as fit as Denning."

"There's a sort of physical assertion about it — do you think that's why it was chosen?"

"Maybe. He is proud of his physical fitness — did you notice that? Not conceited, like the bodybuilding freaks, but quietly pleased to be in peak condition."

"Even for someone in peak condition, even when the victim is a not-young woman, even then strangling is a dodgy business. . . . It's almost as if he wanted a slow way, wanted Lydia to suffer, wanted her to know what was happening to her and recognise him."

"That's nonsense. She didn't know him. She got it all wrong, because she saw the beard and thought, rather uncertainly, that it must be Robert. But aren't you overlooking the obvious explanation?"

"What's that?"

"That he's something of a sadist. Lawrence was a masochist who had himself beaten. Stanley liked having his blacks flogged. A slow sort of death for his victim would appeal more to a sadist than a quick bullet."

"Maybe," Charlie sighed. The human dimension in this case was troubling him. "I certainly didn't get any feeling of a sadist. But then, as I say, I didn't get the feel of anything . . . I can imagine myself giving evidence in the witness box and looking across at the dock, looking into those eyes. And I'll think: I don't really know you. And he'll know I don't, and it'll be a sort of victory. He'll know I'm ending the case only half understanding."

"That's the name of the game," said Oddie. "Most police work leaves you half understanding."

They finished up their pints and went back to their work of half understanding.

Thea Hoddle was writing a letter. She had been wanting to write it for months but now with Andy back at school and the first chill of autumn meaning a coal fire in the living room, now she really intended to do it. To try. Probably there was no way it could be done, but. . . .

She fetched a little Victorian desk-top that went on her lap, something she had inherited from a mother she had been very fond of, put pad and pen in front of her, then sat thinking. Then slowly, painfully, she began to write.

Dear Mr Denning,

You will be surprised to get a letter from me. Or perhaps not — perhaps you have been wondering whether you would? I have been wanting to write ever since I saw the picture of you and Robert being taken into the magistrate's hearing. I still find the killing of my sister disturbing and shocking, but sometimes I look into my heart and know that it was something I could have done myself, wanted often to do. We all have more cruelty in us than we acknowledge, I think. When Lydia took our children from us she did it with cruelty: she couldn't *just* take them — she wanted her supremacy acknowledged, she wanted our supplanting to be visible to all. I never did forgive her for that.

People *do* do cruel things, don't they, all the time? Some months after the Falklands War was over a man rang me out of the blue. He wanted me to know, he said, that my son Gavin was not dead. He said that in the three days he was in London after he had flown back from Washington — days when we didn't see him, only talked to him on the telephone, and that briefly — he met up in London with a naval lieutenant who had recently left the service. They met over a drink in a pub near the Junior Army and Navy Club, and apparently this former lieutenant was mad with frustration because he was missing the action he had always craved in his service career and never got. And Gavin was racked with doubts about the war, doubts about his role in it, and dread of the sort of war it was going to be, based on his knowledge of the sort of weapons he had been promoting while in Washington.

He said they decided to change places.

This was possible because Gavin had been out of regular service life for more than four years. They knew that someone on the ship would know that this was not Gavin Hoddle, but they thought that this could be kept quiet, especially in the chaos of sudden embarkation for war. The man who phoned me said that two people on the *Sir Galahad* knew of the deception: one was killed the same day as 'Gavin,' and he was the other. He said he was sure my son would contact me soon.

I didn't believe it at the time. I remember crying into the phone, but not really believing him. I didn't tell Andy, because he had been so devastated by Gavin's death, and it seemed cruel to arouse hopes on the basis of what seemed like a very nasty hoax. But perhaps in the back of my mind there was always the hope that just conceivably Gavin was alive, and out there somewhere under a new name, and would make contact.

As I say, people can be cruel.

Now that Andy has a job I sit here a lot on my own, wondering. I wonder how you and Robert met up. I wonder if your plans to murder Lydia were always spoken of merely as a joke (the police say that's what Robert will plead). I wonder about the reading of Lydia's letter, and the feelings that aroused in you. I wonder if Robert will remain silent if he is found guilty.

Above all I wonder, if I asked to be allowed to pay you a visit, if you would consent to see me. . . .

Thea stopped writing. Of course he would not consent to see her. Why would he want to make contact, now of all times? She was hardly even marginal in his life — in that respect, at least, Lydia's victory had been total.

She read through the letter. Of course it could not be sent. Even if she could be sure it would not be read by the prison authorities, it could not be sent. She could not make an approach, where the approach would clearly be unwelcome. She tore the letter into pieces and threw them into the fire. Then she sat looking at the burning coals until Andy came home from school.

The employees of THORNDIKE PRESS hope you have enjoyed this Large Print book. All our Large Print titles are designed for easy reading, and all our books are made to last. Other Thorndike Large Print books are available at your library, through selected bookstores, or directly from us. For more information about current and upcoming titles, please call or mail your name and address to:

THORNDIKE PRESS
PO Box 159
Thorndike, Maine 04986
800/223-6121
207/948-2962